OFFICIAL STATS

NAME:	Zane Russell
VITALS:	Age: 32
	Height: 6'1"
	Eye Color: Blue
	Hair: Black
OCCUPATION:	Government agent
OBJECTIVE:	To bring his mission to a successful close.
ADDITIONAL INFO:	Dedicated protector.

DANGEROUS
TO
LOVE

DANGEROUS TO LOVE
USA

MARIE FERRARELLA
THE AMNESIAC BRIDE

Silhouette Books

Published by Silhouette Books
America's Publisher of Contemporary Romance

To all the readers of romantic fiction, with love,
for making wonderful things happen.

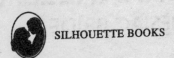

SILHOUETTE BOOKS

ISBN 0-373-82326-6

THE AMNESIAC BRIDE

Visit Silhouette at www.eHarlequin.com

Printed in U.S.A.

MARIE FERRARELLA

earned a master's degree in Shakespearean comedy and, perhaps as a result, her writing is distinguished by humor and natural dialogue. This RITA® Award-winning author's goal is to entertain and to make people laugh and feel good. She has written more than 100 books for Silhouette, some under the name Marie Nicole. Her romances are beloved by fans worldwide and have been translated into Spanish, Italian, German, Russian, Polish, Japanese and Korean.

Books by Marie Ferrarella in Miniseries

Dear Reader,

I have always loved romantic stories with a heavy dose of action-adventure woven through them. *The Amnesiac Bride* is such a story. Picture, if you will, waking up in bed next to a gorgeous man, a man who is a complete stranger to you. Moreover, picture waking up a complete stranger to yourself, with no clues to your existence other than the wedding dress hanging in the closet. That is exactly what happens to Whitney Bradshaw one sunny morning in an exclusive Las Vegas hotel. To complicate matters, nothing is what it seems to be on the surface. I hope you enjoy joining Whitney as she untangles the web around her and finally finds out the truth about her identity. Oh, and as she finds her way, she winds up losing her heart. But then, we rather suspected that would happen all along, didn't we?

As always, I thank you for reading and I wish you love from the bottom of my heart.

Marie Ferrarella

Please address questions and book requests to:
Silhouette Reader Service
U.S.: 3010 Walden Ave., P.O. Box 1325, Buffalo, NY 14269
Canadian: P.O. Box 609, Fort Erie, Ont. L2A 5X3

Chapter 1

She opened her eyes and slowly became aware of a void. A huge, shimmering, all-consuming void that threatened to swallow her up whole and send her tumbling, head over heels, into a gaping abyss that had no end.

The void wasn't outside her, it was within. *She* was the void.

She blinked, attempting not so much to clear her mind but to summon an image, any image, to it.

Nothing.

There was nothing.

With furtive movements, she focused on various items in the large, sun-splashed bedroom, searching. Desperately hoping to see something that would trigger a reaction, a thought. Panic engulfed her.

There wasn't a single familiar thing in it. Not the flower arrangements that seemed to litter every flat surface in the room, not the room itself, or even the half-naked man lying beside her.

The sudden realization that she wasn't alone made her bolt upright in bed, her body rigidly alert. The gasp that rose in her throat was stifled by a will that wasn't quite her own. Instinct, for lack of a better word, seemed to be taking hold. She allowed it to govern her. It was all she had.

Lips pressed together, she stared at the sleeping man. Again there was nothing. He triggered no memories. How was that possible? How could she not remember who this man lying in bed next to her was?

At that moment, a horrible realization encompassed her. She didn't know who she was.

She didn't know her own name.

There was no name to grasp, no murky syllables to try to piece together into a whole. There was nothing. Only the void. And this room, this man.

She was more stunned than afraid. Real fear hadn't had time to register yet. It hovered just on the rim, waiting to embrace her with its icy arms.

Who was he? And why was he sleeping on top of the covers instead of beneath them?

Quickly, she leaned forward to look at him more carefully before he woke up and perhaps asked questions of his own. Questions she couldn't answer.

He was wearing faded jeans that, even in sleep, adhered to him like a second skin. The snap was open just below his navel, resting against a taut, flat stomach. He looked to be tall and he was lean and well muscled. There was a definition to his biceps that even his relaxed state couldn't erase. They matched the sharp contours of his face, what she could see of it. One arm was thrown back against his forehead, obscuring a clear view. His hair was dark, almost black, and appeared to extend down to his shoulders in this pose.

He was a complete stranger.

Smothering a frustrated, uneasy sigh, she eased her legs out from beneath the covers. Still watching his face, she rose. He didn't move.

But the room did. It tilted abruptly as a searing pain speared her temple. Caught off guard, she almost crumpled to the floor. She grasped for the bedpost. Snagging it like a pop fly, she wrapped her fingers around the wood and steadied herself. The room righted again. Within a moment, her knees felt stronger.

Afraid she'd woken him, she looked quickly at the man on the bed. He was still asleep. Relief trickled through her veins. She didn't want to deal with the man yet. Not until she had some sort of handle on all this.

Some sort of name to attach to herself.

Cautiously, she moved toward the mirrored closet. The reflection looking back at her was that of another stranger. A stranger with wide, lost blue eyes and long blond hair that fell razor straight against her bare shoulders. The ends flirted with the edge of a turquoise nightgown that was short on material and long on dreams. The woman in the mirror was almost hauntingly pretty. She didn't remember being pretty.

For a moment, she could only stare at the reflection, wondering who the woman was. Wondering how she got here, to this state.

A breeze from the partially opened window ruffled the gauzy material. It fluttered and moved about her. She felt cold. There had to be a robe around somewhere.

With hands she fought to keep from shaking, she slowly opened the closet door. Maybe she could find a robe inside.

Her hand tightened on the door.

There was a robe in there, all right. It was hanging beside a wedding gown. Not a dress, but a gown in the full sense of the word. An exquisite gown with appliqué and beading that suggested the outrageously huge price tag that had once been attached to it. A few grains of rice were on the carpet just below the hem.

A sense of awe fluttered through her as she reached out to touch the gown. Was it hers?

She looked over her shoulder toward the bed. And did he go with it?

Her heart began to hammer wildly as the full impact of the situation took root.

She pulled the white robe from its hanger and quickly put it on. Just as quickly, she searched each pocket, hoping for a clue. Her fingers curled around something glossy in the left pocket.

She was conscious of holding her breath as she pulled her hand out.

It was a photograph, a Polaroid taken of her and the man in the bed. Except that he didn't have jeans on. He was wearing a tuxedo. The kind men wore when they married women in gowns with high price tags. Gowns like the one she was wearing in the photograph.

Panic began to nibble away at her. If she knew all that, if she knew about gowns and tuxedos and Polaroid photographs, the question echoed in her lonely brain, why didn't she know who she was? And why couldn't she remember posing for this picture?

Tears began to moisten her lashes as she stared down at the photograph in her hand.

"Hey, you're up."

The unexpected greeting startled her. She swung around toward the source, something defensive snapping into place and galvanizing her spine. It was all automatic, done without conscious thought.

Something told her she didn't trust strangers and despite the photograph in her hands, he was a stranger. At least for now.

"Looks that way," she replied guardedly.

Zane Russell pulled his body upright on the bed and leaned against the headboard. He had sat up most of the night, watching her, because he'd been concerned. It had been a hell of a night.

Body aching, he rotated his shoulders, stretching them subtly, like a tiger waking from a half sleep. How had it gotten to be morning so soon?

Making the best of it, he dragged one hand through his hair, then rubbed it across his face, brushing sleep aside. He could snap into action at a moment's notice but enjoyed the luxury of not having to do that now. He could relax around Whitney the way he couldn't afford to around too many people.

He glanced toward her now. Was it his imagination, or was she looking at him oddly? She'd certainly had him worried for a while there, but it looked as if everything was all right.

The itch at the back of his neck warned him that maybe he was being too optimistic too soon. It wasn't something he was in the habit of doing very often.

Zane looked at her again. Her expression puzzled him. Her body language only compounded it. She seemed tense, like a diver on the edge of the board before a major dive. A diver who wasn't sure the pool had been filled with water.

"How do you feel?"

When he rose and moved toward her, she took a step back, her eyes on his face. It wasn't a face that a woman would easily forget. Yet she had. Completely. Why? What had happened to her?

The words in response to his question came out slowly, rolling toward him one at a time. "How am I supposed to feel?"

Zane's brows almost touched as they drew together. She was being unusually cagey this morning. And it wasn't his imagination. She *was* looking at him oddly. What was going on?

"I don't know." He shrugged. "You tell me." How had this turned into a debate? And was she trying to maintain a distance between them?

Subconsciously testing his theory, he reached out for her arm. Whitney backed away. The look on her face said she didn't know if he was going to touch her or strike her. What the hell was wrong with her? He thought of last night. Maybe they weren't out of the woods yet.

His eyes daring her to move, he took another step toward her. "That was a pretty nasty bump you got last night."

"Bump?"

She echoed the word, letting it play across her mind. It meant nothing to her, brought back no scene, no sensation. She held perfectly still, afraid to breathe, as his tentative fingers felt around her forehead. Only when the man brushed against the bump did she wince and pull her head back.

Zane dropped his hand to his side, staring at her. The swelling had gone down, just as the doctor had told them it would. Everything was supposed to be all right now.

"Yeah, bump." He studied her face. "The one you got—hey, what's with you this morning, Half-Whit?"

He'd once seen a look that had passed through a

child's eyes as she tried to grasp the string of a balloon that the wind had ripped from her hands, only to miss. Whitney had that same look in her eyes now. His uneasiness grew.

"What?" he pressed.

Disappointment filled the void, choking her, then disappeared without a trace. She was empty again.

She shook her head. She could almost hear it rattling. "Nothing. Only for a minute, I thought that sounded familiar."

What the hell was she talking about? "Of course it sounded familiar. I've been calling you that for..."

His voice trailed off as he took a closer look at her. Impatience dropped from him like a snake's outer skin. She didn't look like herself at all. The jaunty, devil-may-care confidence was gone. And he couldn't put a name to what was in its place. He only knew he didn't like what he saw.

Something in his gut turned over.

Zane took hold of her shoulders. She was trembling. It wasn't cold in the room. He looked into her eyes and saw nothing except a tiny spark of fear. The woman he knew was gone.

His voice was low and deadly calm as he asked, "What's the matter?"

Somehow it seemed cowardly to admit it. She had a vague feeling that she wasn't a coward. That made her feel a little better, though why it should, she couldn't say. She couldn't say a lot of things.

She had the oddest feeling that she had leaped into this body from nowhere. Leaped into it like...like that scientist in the TV show.

Hysteria bubbled and receded, held back by a steely lid she clamped down on it. My God, she had no idea who she was, or where she was, and yet she remembered a TV program. It made no sense.

Nothing made any sense.

She raised her eyes to the man in front of her. Could she trust him? Trust was important to her. She knew that, too. And knew that she had no other choice. She had to trust him. She had to let someone into this solitary world she found herself in.

Hesitating, she wet her lips and took a chance. "I don't know who I am."

"What?" Zane released her and backed away, shaking his head.

Whatever she thought his reaction would be, annoyance hadn't headed the list. But he obviously was annoyed. Very annoyed.

"This is a hell of a time to try to spring a practical joke."

She grasped at the straw he'd unintentionally offered her. "Do I do that? Do I play practical jokes?"

What was she asking him that for? "You know you do." He opened the closet and took out a navy blue pair of slacks. If he had his way, jeans would be the only clothing anyone would wear, but there were certain requirements to this game. He took a shirt out that was the color of corn bleached by the sun. That ought to do it. "Now hurry up, we have to be—"

He stopped talking as he turned to look at her over his shoulder. She was still standing there, in the center of the room, looking like a lost waif.

He'd never seen her like that before. Zane let the clothes drop on the bed.

Instincts he had long ago learned to trust with his life nudged their way forward. "My God, you're serious, aren't you?"

Very slowly, biting her lower lip to keep it from trembling, she nodded. She fought the tears she suddenly felt rising again.

"Yes."

The hoarse response echoed in the hotel suite, the sound framed by the four walls. Beyond the window, seven floors down, the people who flocked to Las Vegas to divert themselves, or to win easy money that turned out not to be so easily wooed, were busy going about their business. They could have been a thousand miles away for all the difference they made.

Stunned, Zane sank down on the bed, his green eyes never leaving her face. If she was lying, he'd know. And if this was a joke, he was going to kill her. Slowly. "You're telling me you have amnesia?"

What did it take to make him understand? "I'm telling you I don't know who I am."

She wasn't kidding. She was serious. *What the hell am I supposed to do now?* he wondered.

She thought he looked more devastated by the revelation than she did and didn't see how that could be possible. But then, if they had just been married...

Her fingers curved around the photograph she'd hastily shoved back into her pocket when he'd woken up. "Are you my husband?"

Thoughts were colliding in his brain like megabytes of information being processed in a computer. The question brought him up abruptly. He looked up at her, surprised.

"What?"

She pulled out the photo and looked at it again, then raised her eyes to his face. "Are you my husband?" she repeated.

For the first time, she looked down at her hand. There

were rings on it. Huge, magnificent rings. The diamond engagement ring gleamed and shot off rays as it trapped a sunbeam within its sphere. The glow reflected off the diamonds encrusted in the gold band beneath it.

Her mouth formed a perfect O as she stared at the light show. The stones were large enough to have their own zip code.

At least one of them, she thought, was very, very rich.

Zane scrubbed his hand over his face. This was going to complicate everything. Why hadn't she been more careful last night? He'd told her to stay in the hotel room, but she had been stubborn and followed him. And then she'd fallen.

The laugh he uttered was purely reflexive, a throwaway sound.

"I'm—" Debating, he made a decision and hoped it wasn't the wrong one. There'd be hell to pay eventually if it was.

Zane moved toward her and put his hands on her shoulders again. Hoping against hope, he looked into her eyes one more time.

No, this wasn't a joke. She'd never carry one this far. Damn it, anyway. He should have locked her up in the room last night. But it was too late for remorse now. He'd have to play the hand he'd been dealt. He always had before. But this time, he had a feeling it was going to be harder than usual to bluff.

A practiced smile slid across his lips. With just the smallest bit of effort, Zane forced it to his eyes. A man did what he had to do to survive. "Yes, I'm your husband."

She had the photograph and the rings, yet his assurance couldn't penetrate the invisible wall wrapped around her. Couldn't nudge a single memory to the fore. She bit her frustration back.

"Then you'd know my name."

His eyes touched her face, her hair, with such familiarity she thought she should remember at least a kernel of something. But she didn't.

Taking her hands in his, Zane nodded. "Yes, I know your name."

Maybe if she heard it. "What is it?" she asked hopefully.

This was going to take some time, Zane thought. And time was the one thing they didn't have in abundance. Not if this thing was going to go off on schedule. But he couldn't just ignore the situation, either. Damn, but this was a mess.

Trying to be as gentle as he could, Zane took her by the hand and sat her down on the bed.

"Your name is Whitney. Whitney Bradshaw." He searched her eyes to see if that made any impression on her.

She could almost feel him delving into her mind, looking for something as hard as she was looking for it herself. Maybe he was her husband. There was no reason to doubt him just because she couldn't remember. Why would he lie?

Powerless to make a connection with the name, she shook her head in response to the unspoken question that hung between them.

All right then, here goes, he thought. "Actually, your name's Whitney Russell now. We were married two days ago in a chapel just outside of Las Vegas. We're in Las Vegas right now. The Hotel Zanadu."

She didn't know a single thing about herself outside the fact that she had, at least once, watched a TV program about a time traveler, yet what he was telling her didn't sound right. Didn't feel right. She didn't think she was the kind of person who would have been happy settling for a ceremony in Las Vegas. Something told her she had more taste than that. More of a sense of tradition.

And then there were the clothes.

Confused, she pulled out the photograph from her pocket and held it up to him again.

"Aren't these very fancy clothes for Las Vegas?" If she was just going to run off with him, why had she bothered bringing such an expensive-looking gown with her?

Zane sighed. Whitney might not be in there at the moment, but she'd left behind her annoying habit of picking things apart. He might have known the worst traits would remain.

"You insisted," he told her, the smile on his lips never fading. "You said you wanted a memorable photograph of your wedding, even if the place wasn't."

"Why Las Vegas?" The rings didn't look fake. The gown certainly wasn't. That meant there was money enough for a huge wedding.

His smile widened. This time, there was just the slightest trace of amusement in his eyes. "You were in a hurry."

In a hurry. That, like the nickname he had called her, almost struck a chord before fading away. She held the photograph in both hands, looking down at it. Willing herself to remember, to grasp the half memory before it became a ghost.

Like sugar in the rain, it was gone.

"Was anyone else there?" She raised her eyes to his.

"My parents? Brothers? Sisters?" She tried to conjure up faces to go with the labels. They didn't come.

He continued to watch her eyes as he answered. "You don't have any."

"Not even...a brother?" Her lips surrounded the word. She'd said it before. *Brother.* To whom?

"You had one," he said quietly, reaching for her hand. "You told me he died."

Died. Someone died. A brother. Her brother.

Whitney sighed. She was alone. That would account for some of the emptiness she felt. But not all. A new-lywed shouldn't feel as if she were hollow. Should she?

"Then there's just you?" she asked Zane, her voice hardly above a whisper.

Guilt raced through him. He squelched it. Mustering the most sympathetic look he could, Zane covered her hand with his own and squeezed it.

"Just me."

She nodded, absorbing the information. "What's your name?"

"Zane. Zane Russell." He could see that didn't mean anything to her, either.

Very lightly, he brushed aside her hair and looked at the bump she'd sustained last night. It didn't look very big now. He'd been concerned enough about it at the time to force her to go to the emergency room even when she'd stubbornly refused. X rays hadn't shown any cause for alarm. There were no signs of a concussion. The doctor had assured him she'd be fine after a night's rest.

Fine. Yeah, right. The man had probably gotten his degree from the back of a matchbook cover.

Zane rose to his feet, his hand still wrapped around

hers. Quinton slept in late. That gave them a few hours' leeway.

"Look, why don't we go back to the hospital?"

Doubt filled the hollow spaces. "Back?"

It was going to be a matter of force-feeding her all sorts of information. He knew the danger in that. He was going to have to be very careful.

Zane nodded. "I took you there last night, after you hit your head. Community General."

The name meant less than nothing to her. "How did I happen to...?"

He anticipated her question. The scenario was one he'd thought of last night, while driving her home from the hospital. In case anyone should ask.

"In the pool. The one on the roof. It was late, and we had it to ourselves. I guess we got a little carried away," he said vaguely, then flashed her a dazzling smile when he saw more doubt in her eyes. "After all, we are on our honeymoon. Anyway, you slipped and hit your head on the side of the pool."

Had they been skinny-dipping? The way he phrased the explanation made her think that they might have been. She tried to picture that in her mind and couldn't. The tinge of embarrassment rose up to color her cheeks, anyway. She put it out of her mind. There were more important concerns to deal with.

"Was I unconscious?"

"No, that's why you resisted."

"Resisted? You?" That seemed hardly likely. She might not remember Zane Russell, but there was no denying that something within her remembered the chemistry between them. Even now, highly confused and disoriented, she was aware of it. Aware of an underlying strong pull between them.

It was all she needed to convince her that he was telling the truth. Whether or not she remembered it, she was his wife.

"No, going to the hospital. I had to force you to go to the emergency room."

Again, something vague whispered along the perimeter of her mind. Someone being ushered into a car. Was it her? Was he the one doing the ushering? Her head began to ache again.

"You forced me," she repeated.

Despite the gravity of the situation, his mouth curved. "You're stubborn."

So what exactly did she have here? A name and a face, neither of which were even vaguely familiar. And a few scraps of information. How did it all fit together?

"I'm stubborn and I play practical jokes and I have no family." She blew out a deep breath. "Not much to build on, is it?"

Zane thought of his own background. "Some have had less." He wished he could tell her more, but now wasn't the time. Instead, he slipped his arm around her. "C'mon, get dressed and we'll see what the doctor has to say."

Before she could answer, there was a sharp knock on the door.

Chapter 2

The rapid knock came again.

"Room service," a baritone voice on the other side of the door sang out.

Zane hadn't ordered anything.

He looked at the door, then glanced over his shoulder toward the closet, debating. There wasn't time for that. Besides, it would raise too many questions. Her questions.

Zane made no move to open the door. "I didn't send for room service."

"No, sir. Compliments of Mr. Richard Quinton, sir," the voice on the other side of the door cheerfully told him. "He left orders last night to bring you the biggest, best breakfast our kitchen has to offer."

"Oh." Some of the tension left his shoulders. But when Whitney reached for the doorknob, Zane caught her by the wrist. She looked at him, growing steadily more confused. He shook his head, moving his body between her and the door. "I'll get it."

Her head still felt incredibly fuzzy, but Whitney was certain that she'd seen a warning glance pass over his face just as he'd grabbed her wrist. Why was he being so cautious? It was only room service. It just didn't make any sense.

But then, nothing did.

Whitney moved to the side, watching Zane. He opened the door a crack, then a little farther, before finally stepping aside.

Her attention was drawn away from Zane to the cart the bellman was pushing in before him. The top of the mobile table was completely filled with covered dishes. There was just barely enough room for their place settings. Even the empty coffee cups were placed in the center of the plates.

The bellman wheeled the cart over near the window. With a flourish, he began uncovering the various dishes while slanting an appreciative look toward Whitney. There were hot cakes, waffles, sausages, bacon, toast, ham and eggs prepared two different ways. When he was finished, the bellman handed Zane a note.

Unfolding it, Zane found that it said simply, "Eat hearty. Richard Quinton."

Curious, Whitney stood on her toes and read the words over Zane's shoulder. She looked back at the array of hot food.

"Who's Richard Quinton?"

Tossing the note aside, Zane slipped the bellman a five-dollar bill he pulled out of his jeans and then closed the door on the younger man. The sash on Whitney's robe had come undone and her robe was hanging open. It was evident that the bellman had been desperately angling for a better view. Not that Zane could blame him.

He crossed to the cart and picked up one of the empty plates.

"Somebody whose life I saved yesterday." There was comfort in the fact that though the title had been temporarily obscured, Zane could still read Whitney like a book. He saw the question in her eyes. "We were on the golf course. Quinton and the woman with him—Sally, I think he said her name was."

Zane knew damn well what her name was, knew everything that was necessary to know about the pair, down to the size of their underwear and where they went to school. He'd always prided himself on being thorough, but there was no point in saying that now. It would only generate more questions.

"They were playing ahead of us," he continued. "Rather slowly, I might add."

He helped himself to only the toast, taking two servings of raspberry jam to go with it. "Anyway, suddenly this car comes out of nowhere, barreling down the slope. Someone must have forgotten to put on the emergency brake."

Zane poured coffee into a cup, then pushed it toward her. Turning the second cup over, he filled it to the brim. He liked his coffee black and hot, and strong when he could get it. This looked more like tea. Weak tea at that.

"And?" Whitney prompted.

"And if I hadn't pushed him out of the way, Richard Quinton would have died on the thirteenth hole holding a nine iron in his hand."

He said it so simply, as if he was accustomed to saving people's lives on a regular basis. Was he? Was he a fireman or a doctor? Somehow she didn't think so. She studied him as she picked up her coffee cup. The aroma was vaguely tempting. She sipped and frowned, then poured in cream. The aroma was deceptive.

"Looks like yesterday was a busy day." Unconsciously, she touched her forehead for emphasis. "Too bad I can't remember it."

Zane perched on the arm of the sofa and ate. The toast was dark and crisp, just the way he liked it.

"You will," he reassured her.

At least he sure as hell hoped she would. He didn't want to think about the alternative right now. If he had no control over it, it made no sense to dwell on it until he could come up with a plan.

Zane nodded toward the cart. "I guess the kitchen hasn't heard about cholesterol yet." He watched her fill her plate. Whitney was taking something from each dish. "Hungry?"

She hadn't realized she was until the cart had been brought in. At the sight of the food, she had felt her stomach tightening and twisting into a knot, growling. It was as empty as her head. But this at least she could do something about.

Whitney looked up from the plate, placing her hand protectively over the side to keep the sausages from falling off.

"Yes, very."

Zane picked up his last piece of toast. "Well, that hasn't changed any. You always ate like a horse." The assessment wasn't flattering, but it was accurate. His eyes washed over her silhouette. As long as he'd known Whitney, there hadn't been an ounce of excess fat on her. "Near as I can figure it, it changes into pure energy the minute it passes your lips. Same principle as an old-fashioned steam engine."

She knew what he said was true, even if she couldn't remember anything specific to confirm it. Even now, confronted with this all-encompassing hole in her memory, she could feel adrenaline beginning to build. Adrenaline accompanied by an insatiable curiosity.

"I'm active?"

Zane grinned. Here, at least, he was on safe ground. The word active didn't even begin to cover it. "Indefatigable."

She liked that, liked the description a lot better than being told that she ate like a four-legged creature who lived in a stable.

The grin on his face struck a distant chord, like a church bell being rung in a neighboring town. She liked his grin, liked the way it seemed to ripple straight under her skin. The way he was looking at her made her wonder if he meant indefatigable to apply to everything, or if he was referring to something specific.

Something sexual.

Had they slept together before they'd gotten married? she wondered. Or was this honeymoon a virgin run?

The thought brought a smile to her lips, but she didn't ask. Some questions were going to have to be worked up to.

Zane rubbed his thumb over his fingers, getting rid of the crumbs. What was going on in that head of hers? He would have sold his soul to know. Or at the very least, leased it.

Zane set the plate back on the table. She was still looking at him. "What?"

There was so much to learn, so much to experience all over again for the first time. A myriad of possibilities began to suggest themselves to her. She had a feeling that she was accustomed to making the best of things.

"I think that I'm going to have fun finding out about me."

If this were the old Whitney talking, he knew he would be in for trouble. But it wasn't, so maybe he'd have some slack cut him. Heaven knew he was going to need it.

"It'll be an experience," he promised. Zane dusted off his hands on the back of his jeans and rose. "Well, I've had my fill." She was still working her way through her plate. And would probably have seconds, he guessed. "You finish up. I'm going to take a shower and then we're going to see that doctor."

Whitney watched him walk out of the room. She couldn't shake the impression that though it was subtly done, he was rushing her. But why? They were on their honeymoon. Weren't honeymoons supposed to be leisurely?

Shrugging, she finished off what was left on her plate. She supposed that he just wanted to get her to the doctor to have her checked out. Maybe he was hoping the doctor could offer an explanation and some sort of course of action to bring her memory back.

God, she hoped so. She hated this feeling of not knowing anything. Of being only vaguely aware that she had had a life before this morning.

Whitney looked down at her left hand and then toward the closed bathroom door. From the looks of it, and him, it must have been some life at that.

Feeling pleasantly full, she pushed the cart back and rose, then crossed to the closet. She had to find something to wear.

Sliding the hangers along the pole as she took inventory, she noticed that she seemed to favor feminine-looking things. Somehow that didn't feel right, but it obviously had to be, since that was all there was on her side of the closet.

She would have rather worn jeans. Faded ones like Zane's.

Sighing, she selected a straight white skirt and a cherry red pullover. Listlessly, she tossed them on the bed.

Whitney glanced toward the bathroom. The water in the shower was still running. An entire battalion of questions was running through her head. A few were inching their way forward to the top of the list.

One in particular.

If she hesitated, it was only for a second. Since she had no past to fall back on, there was no time like the present. Opening the door, Whitney stood on the threshold for a moment.

The thought that she was standing on the threshold in more ways than one whispered in her mind.

An unfamiliar anticipation began to drum through her as she looked at the stall. A light, foggy haze had risen, partially obscuring the frosted glass and the man within. It was just enough to mute the details of Zane's outline. Mute them, but not erase them entirely. And certainly in no way negate the effect they had on Whitney.

Catching her lower lip between her teeth, she moved toward the shower stall.

He sensed he wasn't alone a second before the shower door opened. Turning, Zane raised his hand defensively. It dropped to his side as surprise paralyzed him. Whitney was standing there, looking almost as surprised as he was. And she was staring at him. Staring and smiling.

He wasn't sure he'd ever seen that smile on her face before. And didn't have a single idea how to interpret it. Belated reflexes had him pulling the door out of her hand and shutting it.

"Just what the hell do you think you're doing?" he demanded.

She thought that was rather obvious. What wasn't exactly obvious, at least not to her, was what had prompted her into the bathroom in the first place. But she was certainly glad she'd come. "Looking at my husband. I was just, um, curious."

Oh, boy. Zane turned up the hot water. The steam wasn't forming nearly fast enough to satisfy him. He attempted to sound nonchalant. "I've got all the working parts, if that's what you mean."

"Zane, are you being shy?" It didn't seem possible, not with a body like that. Not when they were married. Yet he had definitely seemed uncomfortable to her.

She wasn't leaving. Giving up, Zane dragged the bath towel from the side of the stall, shutting off the water simultaneously. He quickly wrapped the towel around his middle and secured it.

"I'm being in a hurry," he corrected, stepping out onto the mat. "Emergency rooms are notorious for long waits. I want to get there as soon as possible. You don't want to waste the whole day sitting on an uncomfortable plastic chair, do you?"

"No." Fascinated, she watched drops of water negotiate a path down the lightly haired expanse of his chest. Several had already made it down, pooling in his navel. She felt a pleasant sensation wash over her.

There was no logical reason why she suddenly felt that things were going to be all right, but she did.

Raising her eyes from his waist and the towel settled snuggly along his hipline, she began to back out of the steamy enclosure.

"I guess I'd better get dressed," she murmured. His clothes, she noticed, were hanging behind the door.

"Good idea." He urged her out. "I'll be with you in a minute."

"Sure." She found herself facing a closed door. There was a click on the other side, telling her that he had flipped the lock.

Who would have thought that someone like Zane would be shy? Maybe they hadn't slept together before they'd gotten married, after all.

And maybe the wedding night had set off fireworks for her. That would explain why she felt her body humming at the sight of his, fleeting though it had been. Her body had a memory, even if she didn't.

Whitney searched through the bureau drawers until she found the one with her undergarments. Preoccupied, she got dressed. She wished there was some instruction booklet she could turn to, something that could make this easier for her somehow. She felt as if she was groping around in the dark.

Of course, she had to admit, from what she'd seen, groping might not be so bad.

Despite the dark side of the situation she found herself in, Whitney felt a smile creeping over her lips as she finished getting dressed.

After all, things could be worse.

The emergency-room waiting area of Community General was crowded with people waiting to be seen by the resident on call. Though he didn't say anything, she could feel Zane's impatience as he took in the scene.

Whitney caught Zane's arm. "Maybe we should come back later," she suggested.

There didn't seem to be much of a reason to wait

around, anyway. She'd actually come more to see if something looked familiar to her from the other night than to be examined again. She had a sinking feeling the doctor wasn't going to be able to do anything for her.

Zane wasn't about to leave. "Later's no good. We're here now," he added before she could ask him why later presented a problem. Zane nodded toward one of the last available chairs. "Sit down over there. I'll be right back."

Leaving her, Zane crossed to the woman at the out-patient desk. From where she sat, Whitney could see that the woman was busy with another patient. Zane leaned over the desk and whispered something into the woman's ear. The receptionist's response was short and terse. The discussion ended there.

Turning from the desk, Zane waved for Whitney to join him. She crossed to him, wondering if the receptionist was going to ask her for some information she wouldn't be able to provide.

Zane took her arm and ushered her to the side. He lowered his voice. "The doctor'll see us in a couple of minutes."

As he said it, an orderly came out to bring them to a small room off to the side of the admission desk that was reserved for private consultations.

Whitney stared at Zane. They had just gone ahead of a roomful of people.

"What did you say to her?"

Zane ran his hand along the back of his neck. His damp hair was just beginning to dry. It curled at the nape of his neck. He wished the itchy feeling would go away, but it persisted. It probably would until this was all over, he guessed.

He grinned as he spared her a glance. "You'd be surprised how many doors the words 'malpractice suit' can open.''

Her eyes widened. ''You threatened them?''

Zane frowned. When he did, she noticed that all his charm turned into glinting steel. ''It's not a threat, it's more like thinking out loud. A definite possibility to consider. The doctor told me that you'd be fine. That you *were* fine. Not remembering your own name isn't fine in my book.''

The momentary anger she saw rise in his eyes held her at bay. There was an aura of danger about him she hadn't detected before. She began to suspect that Zane Russell was not a man to trifle with.

The physician on call, Dr. Kellerman, a harried-looking man in his late forties, tugged at the stethoscope that was slung around his neck. It was a habitual gesture, born of frustration and a sense of impotence. He'd been unable to answer the questions posed to him to anyone's satisfaction, least of all his own.

Kellerman shook his head. When he looked at Whitney, his eyes were full of genuine sympathy.

''We're stumbling around in the dark with amnesia, if you forgive the comparison.'' He was relieved when Whitney nodded. ''There's no certainty when it comes to amnesia.'' He avoided looking at the man on his left. ''Its selectivity isn't something we can even explain. You could remember everything tomorrow—or not.''

Whitney didn't like the sound of that. ''When you say 'or not,' just how long a period of time are we talking about?''

Dr. Kellerman spread his hands helplessly. They weren't dealing with an exact science here. ''Any length of time.''

Whitney could feel the air backing up in her lungs.

Having Zane to occupy her mind with, she'd temporarily pushed the severity of the situation aside. It glared at her now like a cold, cruel specter. She hazarded a guess. "Like a year?"

Kellerman inclined his head. It would be cruel to let her think there was some predictable end in sight. "Or—"

Zane jumped on the word. "Or forever?"

He knew before he asked what the answer would be and silently cursed it. There was no one to blame but himself, he thought. Even if he couldn't have foreseen this, he was still to blame. He should have found a way to make her stay in the hotel room. It had been necessary for only one of them to go. Damn Whitney and her competitiveness.

The question made Kellerman uneasy, but he had to be honest. A doctor owed a patient that.

"Yes." He saw the color drain out of the woman's face. "But the odds are against it," Kellerman added hurriedly.

"Odds. I guess this is the city for it," Zane muttered. A bitter taste rose up in his throat. He swallowed it back.

Kellerman brightened at what he took to be a shred of optimism.

"That it is." He enveloped Whitney's hand in paw-like hands that had precluded his ever picking up a surgical scalpel. They might not be skilled at surgery, but they could offer comfort. "And your wife appears to be very healthy in all other respects."

There was a knock on the door, cutting him short. He knew other patients were waiting to see him. Kellerman leaned on the doorknob.

"I'm sure that this will eventually pass." His eyes shifted to Zane's face. "Just try to be reassuring and supportive. Talk about things that are familiar to her. I'm afraid that it's a wait-and-see situation.''

Zane hated playing waiting games. He'd never been very good at them, even when the stakes were high, but there was obviously nothing else he could do except wait.

He stopped the doctor as he was leaving. ''Why did it happen like this? I mean, why didn't she lose her memory when she hit her head instead of this morning when she woke up?''

Kellerman shook his head. ''Damned if I know.'' He saw the way the man and woman exchanged glances. The answer didn't satisfy them. They weren't the only ones. ''We've made an awful lot of strides in the past few decades, but there's a lot about the brain that is still a mystery to us.'' He pulled several business cards out of his deep pockets and flipped through them until he found the one he wanted. He offered it to Zane. ''I could refer you to a neurologist here, but he'll probably tell you the same thing I did. You just have to wait.''

Zane took the card, pocketing it. He could tell by the look on Whitney's face that she wasn't eager to see another doctor, not if it meant being told the same thing. He couldn't say that he blamed her.

Kellerman crossed the threshold, then paused, as if suddenly remembering.

He hesitated. ''About that lawsuit…''

There was no point in making the man twist in the wind. ''There won't be one,'' Whitney told him.

Zane looked at her, surprised. Well, that hadn't changed. Whitney always liked to take charge of things. That was her problem. And right now, it became his, as well.

''We'll be in touch,'' he told the doctor, negating her

assurance. When Whitney opened her mouth to protest, he placed his arm around her and ushered her through the waiting area. "You never know, we might need to come back here," he whispered firmly, stilling the question on the tip of her tongue. "This'll give us an edge, so that we don't have to wait forever."

She supposed he knew best. Right now, he was the only one who knew anything, she thought darkly. With a sigh, she walked out through the electronic doors ahead of him.

Outside, she looked up at the sky. There wasn't a single cloud to be seen. It was crystal clear, with a sky so blue, it made her soul ache.

For now, she supposed that she should be content just to be alive and married to a man who looked to be a twelve on anyone's one-to-ten scale.

Making the best of it, Whitney surprised Zane by threading her arm through his. "All right, now what?"

He brought her over to the car. "Now we get back to the hotel." Zane opened the passenger door and held it as she got in.

That didn't sound very romantic, or very interesting. She waited until Zane got in on his side and started up the car. "Isn't there someplace else we could go?"

Zane inserted the token that the woman at the desk had given him into the slot at the gate. The striped security barrier rose to let them pass.

"Like where?"

"I don't know." She shrugged, feeling restless. "It seems so lovely out, and I thought that maybe we could go somewhere and just talk."

He guided the car into the moderate traffic. "We can talk at the hotel. Besides, we're meeting Richard Quinton at one." Zane glanced at the digital numbers on the dashboard. It was just past noon.

"Our breakfast benefactor," she recalled. It wasn't difficult to remember that when there wasn't much in the way of thoughts in her mind.

Zane nodded without looking at her. "That's the one."

She shifted in her seat to look at him. "I know that I'm kind of new at this, at everything, actually, but shouldn't newlyweds be alone?"

Was she going to give him trouble after all? "This isn't the town for being alone. Besides, we have lots of time to be alone later." Glancing in her direction, Zane was unable to read the look on her face. "Anyway, the more people there are around you, the more chances that something someone says might bring back your memory, or at least jog it."

"I suppose."

She sounded unconvinced. He didn't have the time to argue about this. Since there wasn't anything they could do about her memory, he was going to keep her in the dark for now. And hope that the light didn't come on at the wrong time.

He changed the topic. "How do you feel?"

"You mean other than the fact that my mind feels like this huge shapeless snowbank?"

It had to be hell for her. "Yeah, other than that."

She shrugged, thinking. "Fine. Nothing seems to hurt. Even the headache's gone."

"Good."

They were talking like strangers. It was time they communicated more like a husband and wife. "Listen, I've got a lot of questions—"

"Fire away." Zane braced himself as he took a corner. Her headache might have abated, but he had a feeling that his was just beginning.

Chapter 3

There were so many questions buzzing through her mind, swarming like bees at the entrance of a hive. Whitney didn't know where to start. Maybe the beginning would be a good place.

"How did we meet?"

Amid gunfire.

Instantly, the image rose up in Zane's mind, crystal clear and sharp, allowing him to relive the first time that he had ever laid eyes on her face.

A smile tugged on his lips. Strictly speaking, that wasn't exactly an accurate description. The first thing he got a glimpse of was not her face but her rear end. She'd backed into him to get out of the way of a spray of bullets. As he recalled, even in all the excitement, he'd been struck by just what a nice tight little butt it was. The rest of her hadn't turned out to be a disappointment, either.

He stopped as three elderly women began making

their way across the street in the center of the block. They walked in small, leisurely steps, as if secure in the fact that since they had lived this long, nothing was about to change that. Probably on their way to play the slot machines, he thought.

"Through mutual friends," he finally told her.

The answer was deliberately vague. The mutual friends they had he couldn't talk about at the moment. He had to keep this simple. To lead her through the maze that actually existed in hopes that she would remember something might place everything he'd worked for in jeopardy.

He wasn't exactly a font of information, Whitney thought. Maybe they'd met a long time ago and he couldn't remember.

"What were their names?" she prodded.

Names, she wanted names. Glancing around the long boulevard, he saw a billboard announcing a headlining act that was opening at one of the hotels on the first of the month. She was looking at him and not the road. He took a chance.

"Cassidy. Joe and Aimee Cassidy," he elaborated. Zane prayed she wouldn't quiz him on this later. He wasn't all that good at names unless his life depended on it. And even then, he'd been known to slip. "They were giving a New Year's Eve party." Taking his foot off the brake as the last of the women reached the opposite curb, Zane got into his story and embellished. "I kissed you to ring in the new year."

That sounded romantic, she mused. Was he a romantic? He didn't quite seem like one, although, she mocked herself, how would she know?

"How long ago?"

"This year." He looked at her ring. "It was something of a whirlwind courtship."

"Then we liked each other right away?" She didn't see how it could have been otherwise, at least as far as she was concerned. Zane exuded a tantalizing, almost dangerous sexuality that she knew she must have found instantly attractive. She did now. It seemed to cut through everything, like a dark marker underlining every word in a paragraph.

They'd clashed immediately, Zane thought. It had been a duel for control right from the start. At times it still was. In a way, it was what made things exciting. But he wished he'd won the battle last night.

Shooting through the light just before the amber color turned red, he nodded.

"You might say there were instant fireworks." At least that much was true.

Whitney was unaware of nodding to herself. That sounded right. "I kind of had a feeling."

Zane raised a brow. "Why?"

Whitney shifted beneath the restraining seat belt, her body all but twisted toward his. She had one foot tucked beneath her. A habit, Zane thought, her body obviously remembered even if she didn't.

"Because I feel it now," she told him. She saw no reason not to be honest.

"Really?" It was hard to keep the grin from surfacing, but he didn't want her to think he was laughing at her. Was she ever going to hate him once she remembered everything! Still, he had to admit that it was tempting to let this line of conversation go on just a little bit longer.

"And what is it exactly that you feel?" Zane tried his best to look as innocent as possible.

She combed both hands through her hair and then let it fall. There was a restlessness in her. She could almost feel it growing. That, and a pull. A huge, powerful pull. Toward Zane.

"I guess they'd call it chemistry." She thought about it for a second. There was a freedom in knowing she was married. "I'm glad we're married and there doesn't have to be any game playing, because I find you awfully sexy." He wasn't saying anything. Was that typical? She laid her hand on his arm and he slanted a look at her before looking back at the road. Zanadu was just ahead. "Don't you find me attractive?"

Yeah, he did. Very. But he'd learn to live with it. It only clouded things. He didn't turn to look at her. "That goes without saying."

He answered the way she would have imagined a man who had been married for a long time might. But they had just gotten married and she wanted more. She tried to make him understand.

"Right now, nothing goes without saying." Whitney paused, waiting. He didn't seem to be very quick on the uptake. "Say it," she whispered.

Lies always came easily to him. That was a matter of necessity. It was the truth he had trouble with. "I find you attractive."

She sighed. He didn't understand what she needed to hear. "Not that."

Her memory might be gone, but she certainly hadn't forgotten how to be a pain in the butt. Zane curbed his impatience. At the same time, he realized that he was a great deal tenser than he was happy about, and it didn't exactly have to do with what he was working on.

"Then what?"

"Say that you love me." She knew that she was almost begging him to tell her, but right now that didn't matter. Pride took second place to need. "I think I need to hear it."

She didn't think, she knew. She needed to hear it, to believe it, because more than anything, she needed something to cling to, to work with. A foundation on which she could build. Knowing that he loved her would give her that beginning.

He'd never said it to anyone—not those exact words, anyway. He'd implied it and let women draw their own conclusions, but the words themselves had never actually left his lips.

He knew that if he would ever have said them, it would have been to her.

Irritation joined hands with impatience. Some of it, he knew, was unreasonable. Zane rubbed his nape, feeling the itch beginning all over again. Glancing at her, he muttered, "I love you."

Disappointed, Whitney frowned. He'd said it with as much feeling as someone asking for an order of fries from a cardboard clown at a drive-through. "You don't sound like you mean it."

"I mean it," he ground out, then felt a shaft of guilt puncture him. She'd just gone through hell, was still going through it. The least he could do was make it a little easier on her. "I don't cue very well, okay? A man picks his own time to say that he loves a woman—at least, I do. That doesn't mean that the feelings aren't there."

There, that should placate her. Then, because it was Whitney, because he really did care about her, Zane added, "I guess I'm just a little tense because I'm worried about you. I've never been faced with a situation I didn't know how to handle before."

She could well believe that. He looked like a man accustomed to having things go his way, or *making* them go his way if necessary. As for saying "I love you," she supposed that some men had trouble voicing their feelings, even to their wives.

She flashed him an apologetic look. "I'm sorry, I guess I'm just being overly anxious right now."

"Small wonder." He blew out a breath. All in all, she was handling this pretty well. "Hell, I don't know how I would react to waking up and finding myself in some strange hotel room without the vaguest idea of who and where I was."

Except for the identity part, there had been a time or three when he had come to in unfamiliar surroundings. But he'd never been stripped of his chief asset—his mind. That would have been very, very difficult for him to come to terms with. That she hadn't broken down just proved what he had already known—that Whitney was one hell of a strong lady.

Zane reached over and covered her hand with his own. "We'll get through this, Whitney. Just hang in there and trust me, no matter what."

What an odd thing to say, she thought. Why shouldn't she trust him? Was there some kind of cryptic message in his words?

Without warning, she suddenly had the eeriest feeling....

But then, just as suddenly, it was gone again before she could grasp it. A wet tissue breaking up in the wind.

Maybe later.

Zane drove the rented car up to the front of the hotel. A tall, strapping valet dressed like a eunuch standing guard in a sultan's harem strode over to them and opened the door for Whitney. It tickled her sense of the absurd.

"Nice outfit," she told the man.

Brilliant white teeth flashed against a dark complexion. "Hey, it's different." The valet held his wide palm out, waiting for keys.

Zane surrendered one of the two sets he always made a point to keep on him. It was one of his idiosyncrasies, but the extras were known to come in handy at times.

Whitney stepped away from the curb and into Zane. As her body brushed against his, she could feel the electricity almost jumping between them. Their eyes met and held for a long moment.

"I picked a hell of a time to lose my memory," she murmured with regret. "On my honeymoon." She raised her face to his. "But it doesn't have to get in the way of things."

"No," he agreed cautiously. What was she up to? "It doesn't."

"We can still have a good time."

He had a feeling that right now their definition of a good time differed drastically. "Yes, I'm sure that we can."

It was almost one o'clock. He had arranged for them to meet with Quinton and his mistress at the ground-level pool at one. They had to get going.

But first, he wanted to take certain precautions. He didn't want to risk things getting fouled up. He placed his hands on Whitney's shoulders, commanding her complete attention.

"Listen, Whit, we have to meet Quinton now. I think it might be for the best if you don't make a big deal about your amnesia."

That was an odd way to put it. He made it sound as if her amnesia was an annoying little inconvenience, like a tiny blemish the night before a date. A minute ago, he'd sounded concerned; now he was trying to sweep it under the rug. Why the sudden change?

"Big deal?" she echoed.

He knew he'd phrased it wrong the minute it was out of his mouth, but he didn't have time to smooth it over for her. Taking Whitney by the arm, Zane walked into the hotel's casino.

"Just don't mention it to them, all right?"

It wasn't exactly something she'd intended to blurt out right after saying hello, but she didn't understand why he wanted her not to say anything at all.

"Why?"

Because it might inadvertently ruin everything. He didn't want either of them questioning her in an attempt to see what they could make her remember. She might remember the wrong thing and blurt it out. He knew he couldn't say that to her without having to explain other things, as well.

"It'll probably make them feel uncomfortable."

She supposed that did make sense. Still...

"Won't they wonder if I don't know the answer to things they might ask me?" There were all sorts of common, everyday things that she had no knowledge of. She looked at him in frustration. "I don't know what my address is, or where I was born." She tried not to let that get to her. "What if they ask me what I like to do in my spare time? What am I going to say? Nothing? They'll think I'm an idiot."

They wove their way through the lobby, heading toward the rear door and the pool beyond. Zane fell back on the truth. "You were born in Washington. Tacoma." And then he began to fabricate. "We live in L.A." He gave her an address that would have checked out if necessary. Probably had been checked out already, he

thought, if what he knew about Quinton was true. "And
you like going to the movies. Everything but horror. You
like comedies best, although you hate slapstick. And
they won't think you're an idiot, although they sort of
have the impression that you're a little, well, scatterbrained."

He had a feeling that wasn't going to go over well
and he was right.

Whitney abruptly stopped walking, nearly bumping
into a waiter carrying a tray full of tall glasses that
looked like a liquid rainbow.

Scatterbrained? That *really* didn't feel right. "Why
would they think I was scatterbrained?"

Because that was what he'd wanted them to think. It
put Quinton off his guard a little. Quinton was accustomed to women being ornamental, remaining in the
background and being easily diverted.

Zane shrugged, making light of it. "You're a blonde
and you talk fast."

Well, she'd seen her reflection. The blonde part was
accurate enough and she did speak quickly, but that was
no reason to come to that conclusion.

"But I'm not."

He didn't want to be late. There was a great deal riding on this meeting and the additional groundwork it
would lay. He gently ushered her in the right direction.
Quinton was visible from here. "Not what?"

He was hurrying. She had to walk quickly to keep up.
"Scatterbrained. Ditzy." Maybe he thought she was.
"Am I?"

There were times when she could think rings around
him. And other times when he could have sworn she had
the mind of a child. But even at her most infuriating, he
would never have said that she was dumb.

Zane shook his head. "No, you're not."

It was a relief to know he didn't think so. "Then why would they think…?"

"People tend to stereotype." He shrugged the matter off. "Look, there they are now."

There were a lot of people in the pool and even more around the perimeter, both in lounging chairs and at the canopied tables that were strategically placed not to interfere with foot traffic. The odds of picking out the right couple were completely against her, especially since she didn't know who she was looking for.

Still, reflexes had her looking around. "Where?"

Zane pointed to the left. "There. The waiter just walked by them.

"Quinton looks a little like the guy who played James Bond. The first one." Zane stopped. "Do you know…?"

She knew what he was going to ask. "Yes, oddly enough, I do know who you're talking about." Even if she was still a mystery to herself.

Whitney looked in the general direction where he was pointing and picked out the waiter, then looked just behind him. There was an older man sitting at one of the larger tables beside a stunning brunette who appeared to be filling out the scarlet sundress she was wearing quite well.

Zane was right—Quinton did look like Sean Connery. Very suave and sophisticated. He was wearing immaculate white slacks and a navy pullover, open at the throat. What looked like a designer insignia was discreetly resting over the single pocket.

As they drew closer to the pair, the scent of a pricey cologne mingled with a whiff of heady perfume and the smell of suntan lotion.

No, a sunblock, Whitney amended. The brunette was fair enough to have passed for Snow White. An X-rated Snow White. The hem of her dress was carelessly gathered around to her thighs. It was an artfully arranged carelessness, Whitney realized, judging by the knowing look on the woman's face.

Whitney shifted her eyes to look at Zane. Was he aroused by women who were well endowed enough for two? In comparison, Whitney felt that she looked like a boy. Her build leaned toward athletic.

Inclining his head, Zane whispered last-minute information into Whitney's ear. "Their names are Richard and Sally."

Sally. The name was far too average to suit the woman. "What is she to him?"

"Ecstasy, probably." Quinton liked his women willing and hot. Sally looked as if she was both. The tennis necklace at her throat, with stones that looked like small robin's eggs, were a testimonial to the fact that she did her job well.

Whitney sniffed. "If you like that sort of thing," she commented, her lips barely moving.

The unabashed display of jealousy tickled him. It wasn't something he would have expected from Whitney. But then, this wasn't really Whitney.

"I'm sure he does."

She had to ask. "Do you?"

Well, she was certainly direct. He'd almost replied that he wouldn't have kicked Sally out of bed but managed to catch himself just in time. Under the circumstances, it wouldn't have been a prudent thing to say.

"I've got you." Zane pressed a kiss to her temple. "Why would I notice anyone else?"

She doubted if any man wouldn't have noticed Sally,

but it was a nice thing to hear. Grateful for the lie, pleased that he'd offered it to her, Whitney stopped just short of Quinton's table. Impulsively, she rose on her toes, framed Zane's face with her hands and kissed him. His surprised expression just before their lips met amused her.

A moment later, Zane knew just what Whitney had to be going through right now. Within seconds of contact, Zane discovered that his head was completely depleted of all thoughts, all memory, everything.

Everything but the cataclysmic effect that her mouth had on his. He could feel his blood heating even as wonder bloomed within his breast. Aroused, curious, he drew her into his arms and let the kiss deepen even further.

Whitney? Was this Whitney? Just what had that bump on her head done to her?

And what was she doing to him?

The chasm below opened wider, letting him complete his free-fall through space and time.

Wow.

The single word said nothing. And everything.

Her body was practically singing as she molded it to his. As her warmth mingled with his. If she'd had any doubts that they were meant to be one, there were none left now.

Biting back a moan, she twined her arms around his neck. This felt wonderful. She felt as if she'd found a piece of herself here, in his arms, in his kiss. The rest of her had to be there somewhere.

She wanted to go up to their suite with him and find it.

Quinton's deep chuckle abruptly returned Whitney to stark reality.

Whitney drew her mouth away from Zane's with a

reluctant sigh. But it took a moment before the throbbing subsided.

The expression on Quinton's lips was more of an appreciative leer than a smile.

"Well, I was just about to give up on you two. Now I see what the delay was." Quinton laughed heartily at his own observation. His smile widened. Despite its breadth, there was something chilly about it, Whitney thought. "I was beginning to think that I'd have to dump the champagne bucket on you two to put out the fire."

Zane stepped away from Whitney, though he kept a proprietary arm around her waist. He shouldn't have let that happen. Pretending to behave like a newlywed was one thing, but he wasn't supposed to get carried away in the part. Reacting to Whitney had been a totally unprofessional lapse on his part. He'd never allowed feelings to interfere with a job before. He was going to have to be careful.

Clearing his head, Zane pulled out a chair for Whitney.

"Sorry, I guess I got a little carried away." That much was true. But it shouldn't have been.

Small, deep-set eyes moved along Whitney's body as Quinton clearly imagined himself in Zane's place. "Can't say I blame you. If I'd just gotten married to her, I wouldn't allow her leave the suite for at least a week." When they narrowed, his gray eyes grew flinty. "The only thing that would interest me would be keeping her naked and happy for as long as possible."

Though the words were meant to be flattering, the breakfast Whitney had consumed threatened to come up. Reluctantly, she took the seat Zane held out for her. She would rather have sat between the woman and Zane instead of beside Quinton, but there was no way to do that without calling attention to it.

"Zane's managing very well." Whitney felt compelled to come to his defense. Or was that her own she was seeing to? She had a feeling that despite the fact that Sally looked like more woman than Quinton could handle, Quinton wasn't the type to be satisfied with a monogamous relationship.

Zane shrugged, taking a seat beside Whitney. "A man's got to come up for air sometime."

More discreet than her companion because she had much more to lose, Sally allowed her eyes to roam over Zane's hard torso.

"You do it too quickly and you might get the bends," she purred. Lips as scarlet as her dress drew back slowly in a smile that was meant to be exactly what it was. Seductive.

Whitney felt her temper rising. That and her hackles. Why did Zane want to be around these people, anyway?

She wished Quinton would stop looking at her like that, as if he were undressing her. And she wished that Zane would *start* looking at her that way. The kiss they'd shared, the first one as far as she was concerned, proved to Whitney that even if Zane might not be vocal about his feelings for her, they were certainly there.

Anticipation began to whisper through her. She turned toward Zane and smiled. She supposed she could put up with this for a while for his sake, since it seemed to mean so much to him. Once they were alone again, she was going to find out why it did.

Uncomfortable with not saying anything, she looked at Quinton. "Breakfast was very good. Thank you."

"Breakfast?" For a moment, Quinton looked at her blankly, then remembered. "Oh, you mean the cart I had sent over.'' He waved her thanks off as less than nothing. "It was the very least I could do, seeing as how I wouldn't be here if it weren't for your husband.''

Quinton frowned, annoyed when he thought of the incident. He didn't believe in accidents. The car hadn't just happened to be there. Someone had meant to kill him.

"I still haven't managed to find out who the car belongs to.'' The plates had turned out to belong to a man who had been dead more than three years. That, too, he knew was no accident. But a man in his position had a great many enemies. It was part of the territory.

Quinton wouldn't find out about the driver anytime soon, Zane thought confidently.

Whitney could understand the other man's impatience. "Sometimes it takes the police a while to track these things down.'' She was relieved that Zane had explained the incident to her. At least she had something to talk about intelligently. She hated feeling out of it, or worse, like a dolt.

"Police?'' The laugh had an amused, if disparaging, ring to it.

Whitney caught the glance Quinton exchanged with Sally. She'd obviously said something funny. Or stupid.

"My dear young woman, why would I bother calling the police in?''

Was this a trick question? "To track down the license?'' Whitney said slowly.

She could see by Quinton's expression that he did think she was lightweight as far as brains went. Whitney could feel her anger rising.

The light in her eyes was not an unfamiliar one to Zane. He placed a gentling hand over hers. It was meant to restrain her if necessary.

"I don't need the police for that," Quinton explained. "I have my own, more effective ways of looking into things."

He regarded her for a moment, as if he was going to say something further, then let it go. Whitney had the distinct impression that he didn't think it was worth the effort.

Instead, Quinton turned his attention to the silver bucket at his side. "Well, enough about unpleasantness. Who would like some champagne?" Not waiting for an answer, he drew the dark green bottle out.

She didn't feel like drinking with them. And certainly not so early.

"It's only one o'clock," Whitney protested.

A tinge of contempt entered Sally's eyes as she offered her glass to Quinton. Rather than fill it, he held the bottle out for Whitney's glass, waiting. "Perhaps here, but it must be midnight somewhere."

She saw the look in Zane's eyes. He didn't want her calling attention to herself. Resigned, she moved her glass forward.

"Yes," she agreed, "I guess it must be."

Chapter 4

Smooth—that was the word for the man. Richard Quinton was handsome, polished, sophisticated and he was knowledgeable on a variety of subjects. The perfect Renaissance man. And yet there was something about him, something Whitney couldn't quite put her finger on, that made her uncomfortable.

Maybe he was too suave. He didn't seem quite real to her.

The man's eyes missed nothing. She could tell. They made her think of the eyes of a sleek jungle cat watching the brush, waiting for prey to emerge. Cold eyes. He was the kind of man she wouldn't have wanted to number among her acquaintances. She wondered why Zane had been so eager to place him there.

They had sat at the umbrella-shaded table for the better part of an hour. Quinton had dominated most of the conversation. Sally barely joined in, except to agree with him in a distracted fashion. Whitney had a feeling Quinton didn't appreciate her manner, though he said nothing. For the most part, it seemed to her that Quinton was sizing Zane up. The fact disturbed her and aroused protective feelings within her.

She thought longingly of an intimate lunch and knew it wasn't going to happen. Zane looked perfectly content sitting here, talking to Quinton. He had the air of someone who had definitely settled in for a long visit. Maybe dinner would be better.

The conversation progressed by stages. As it went from general topics such as weather and accommodations to more specific things, Whitney could see the shift in attitude. Zane became more animated, more involved. He was doing more talking to Quinton than he had to her. Making the best of it, Whitney listened and tried to glean information.

Zane was just beginning to touch on things that piqued her curiosity when one of the costumed bellmen approached their table.

When she saw him, Whitney thought he was a waiter, but there was no menu tucked under his naked, muscular arm. Neither Quinton nor Sally gave any indication of interest in food. Lunch for them, apparently, was of the liquid variety.

The bellman leaned solicitously over Zane, causing the conversation to abruptly halt. "Excuse me, Mr. Russell?" Zane inclined his head in response. "There's a telephone call for you."

Whitney stared at the bellman, surprised that he was able to pick Zane out. There were so many people around the pool; how had he recognized Zane?

Quinton toasted Zane with what was left in his glass. "I'm impressed. They know who you are here." The fact that they did placed Zane in a small, intimate group. The same one that he was in.

Zane casually lifted a shoulder and let it drop. His manner said that this was not anything new or surprising.

"It might be because I'm a large tipper." Quinton, Zane knew, enjoyed having people dance attendance on him in hopes of being rewarded. He looked up at the outlandishly costumed man. "Can you bring a phone to the table for me, please?"

The bellman looked genuinely apologetic. "I'm sorry, sir, but they're all in use at the moment. I'm afraid that you'll have to take the call at the front desk. Or I can take a message for you."

Zane shook his head. "That wouldn't be wise. Not if they think it's important enough to track me down here and disrupt my honeymoon."

They? Who are 'they?' Whitney wondered. And why was someone calling him here? She realized that though she had begun to ask several times, she still didn't know what Zane did for a living. He'd either been interrupted or vague in his response.

Just as he had been about why they had to meet with Quinton.

Zane rose, a resigned expression on his face. "I'll only be a minute," he promised Quinton. Turning toward Whitney, he saw the tiny spark of panic entering her eyes. She didn't want him to leave. He didn't want to leave her alone with these people, either, but it was unavoidable. Adams wouldn't have come looking for him if it hadn't been. Something was up. He'd be as quick as he could.

Zane leaned over her and squeezed her hand. "It's okay," he whispered. His manner more than his words were meant to reassure her. He looked at Quinton before following the bellman. "Why don't you entertain my wife while I'm gone?"

Quinton's smile spread slowly as he looked at Whitney. "I would be honored." The words were polite, harmless. She couldn't have said the same about the look in his eyes.

She was being ridiculous, she upbraided herself. Was she that much of a coward that she needed her husband around constantly to hold her hand?

Zane appeared to already be forgotten as Quinton leaned over the table and took her hand. "So, Mrs. Russell, just how would you like to be entertained?"

It didn't take a clairvoyant to tell her what Quinton would have had in mind, had they been alone.

Zane hurried away, wishing that Sheridan had picked his time better.

Trapped, Whitney decided to turn the situation to her advantage. Maybe she could find out a few things, such as why this man and Zane seemed to have an affinity for each other. She toyed with her glass. "You could tell me what you do for a living."

Quinton's brow rose sharply at the casual remark. Like a miser who had suddenly realized that a nickel was missing from his coffers.

His easygoing tone was in direct conflict with the expression in his eyes. "Now why would you want to know something as boring as that?"

Because I don't have anything to say myself and I can't just sit here like mindless dolt, searching for something to talk about.

From out of nowhere, a movie scenario came to her, and because she had no idea what her own personality was, Whitney slipped into the persona of an actress in a role. She was Audrey Hepburn in *Sabrina*. Elfin and charming. In a pinch, that would do nicely.

Turning the conversation around to Quinton, Whitney leaned forward, her head resting on her upturned palm. She looked at the large gold ring on his hand. There was a square-cut diamond in the center that rivaled hers. She'd already gotten the feeling that Quinton and monetary woes were not acquainted.

"It can't be all that boring if you can afford a ring like that."

Quinton looked at the ring as if he hadn't seen it for quite some time.

For a moment, he watched the sun sparkle on the stone, then shifted his gaze to Whitney's hand. "It pales in comparison to the one on your hand, my dear."

He signaled to a waiter, holding the empty bottle aloft. The message was clear. Satisfied that the waiter understood, he slid the bottle back into the bucket. Ice water splashed over the side.

Quinton cocked his head as he appraised Whitney. "Do you like jewelry, Mrs. Russell?"

She knew that Zane would have wanted her to personalize the conversation and take it to the next plateau, but she couldn't force herself to make the man call her by her first name. Instead, she smiled. "Yes, I do."

Whitney didn't have to be told that Quinton thought all women loved jewelry and clothes. For all his sophistication, he had the air of a man who had pigeonholed women. But for Whitney, the stones on her hand didn't hold any particular interest, other than as a symbol of the bond she had with Zane. She said what she felt Quinton expected to hear. It was easier that way.

She looked at the tennis necklace around Sally's neck. The woman was deliberately fingering it to call her attention to the stones. Whitney saw no harm letting the woman preen.

"That's a beautiful necklace you have."

The smile on Sally's lips was coolly smug. "Yes, I know." Her brown eyes slanted toward Quinton. "It was given to me as a token of appreciation."

The waiter returned with another bottle of champagne, standing to Quinton's right. The smile on Quinton's lips froze. It matched the frost in his eyes.

"My left, you dolt. Hasn't anyone trained you properly? You're supposed to stand on my left."

As if prodded by the point of a sword, the waiter quickly moved to Quinton's other side. The scowl lifted as Quinton took the bottle from him. "That's better."

Sally noticed the confused look in Whitney's eyes. She took pleasure in enlightening her. "Richard has superstitions."

Whitney couldn't quite tell if the fact amused the woman or not. She didn't risk a smile, but her eyes told another story.

"Patterns," Quinton corrected her. "Patterns I see no reason to go against. You change a pattern, you change things that depend on them for an outcome." He looked kindly at Whitney. "Sometimes, however, a change is for the good. Such as you and your husband appearing when you did on the golf course yesterday. You realize, of course, that this makes you my good-luck charms now?"

She didn't know if he was kidding. She had an uneasy feeling that he was very serious, despite the smile on his lips.

Well, this was certainly getting uncomfortable. Whitney glanced around, hoping to see Zane walking toward them. He'd promised to be right back. How many minutes were there in "right back," anyway?

Whitney pushed back her chair. "Maybe I should see what's keeping Zane," she suggested to her host, rising to her feet.

Quinton stopped pouring champagne and caught her hand, his fingers closing around her wrist like a tight-fitting band. Whitney didn't know who was more surprised—she or Sally.

"Surely you don't plan to desert me, as well, do you?" He set the bottle on the table beside his glass as he looked up at her. Whitney tried not to stiffen as she felt Quinton run his thumb along the inside of her wrist. "You know," he began speculatively, "your wrist is quite dainty. It strikes me as being just the right size for a bracelet that has recently come into my possession. Diamond. Five carats." He said the words matter-of-factly as he watched her face. "A client couldn't pay his bill. He tendered the bracelet to me instead. I've been debating what to do with it ever since."

Whitney looked at Sally. Was this the man's way of getting back at the woman for her comment about his having superstitions? Anger glinted in Sally's eyes, but she said nothing.

"I'm afraid my husband wouldn't like that," Whitney informed him politely. "Perhaps you should give it to Sally."

"I'll decide who to give it to."

This was much too uncomfortable for her to endure alone. Slipping her hand from his grasp, Whitney began to back away. "I really think I should see what's keeping Zane. This isn't like him." She had no way of knowing whether it was or not; she knew only that she wanted to get away for a little while. "He really shouldn't keep you waiting like this."

Quinton had never been accused of displaying false modesty. "I'm not accustomed to being kept waiting. Not without entertainment."

There was no way she was going to provide *that* any longer. "I'll be right back," she promised. *When pigs fly,* she thought, if she had her way.

Without sparing either of them a backward glance, Whitney hurried toward the hotel door. Once inside the hotel, she discovered that her mind wasn't the only thing that was disoriented. She had a complete lack of a sense of direction. There were too many people in the way for her to get her bearings. Which way was the front desk?

She stopped the first bellman she saw and asked directions. Repeating them to herself like a chant, she finally arrived at the desk. Her heart sank. Zane was nowhere in sight.

Where had he gone?

Feeling a little desperate, Whitney approached the man behind the reservations desk. "Excuse me, could you tell me where Mr. Russell went?"

Without turning his head, the man raised his eyes from the computer screen. His fingers remained poised on the keys. The smile he offered was both bright and without substance. It was exercised over a hundred times a day. "Who?"

Whitney couldn't shake the edgy feeling wafting through her. It might have originated in her amnesia, but it was steadily growing larger. It was as if everything she came in contact with insisted on contributing to it.

"The man who took a call here."

The clerk looked at her blankly. "I'm afraid you're

mistaken.'' He looked back at the screen and began to type. ''No one took a call at the desk during my watch.''

Whitney leaned over and placed her hand over his, stilling the soft clatter of keys. He looked at her patiently, silently waiting for her to continue.

''The bellman just came for him. At the pool. He said there was a call for my husband.'' Whitney said each word slowly, as if that would make him understand. She could feel her frustration building.

The clerk looked down at her hand and waited until she withdrew it before he replied. His tone was patronizing. ''If there was a call for your husband, the bellman would have brought a telephone to your table.'' He began typing again.

An impatient sigh escaped her lips. ''The bellman said that they were all being used.''

The man ceased typing. His expression never changed as he reached down behind the desk and produced a small telephone. Then he spared her a smile meant for a mentally challenged individual.

''Hardly. I assure you that there are more where that came from.''

She didn't understand, not any of it. Why would the bellman say there were no telephones available if there were? And where was Zane? Why had he just disappeared? There had to be some explanation.

Whitney looked around, feeling a little desperate. ''Is there another front desk somewhere?''

Thinking himself the target of a prank, the clerk's manner became distant. ''Yes. But that would be at another hotel, I'm afraid.''

He wasn't going to be any help. Whitney backed away from the desk as a man in a Stetson ushered a large-boned woman swaddled in a full-length fur coat forward.

The woman appeared to be quite oblivious to the temperature outside.

"We'd like a room," the man announced in a booming voice. "The name's Allen. Kiki and Jordan."

"Make sure they give you a telephone," Whitney murmured to the man as she walked away.

Whitney dragged her hand through her hair. There had to be some mistake. Where could Zane have gone? Everyone couldn't be lying to her, and yet nothing was making any sense.

She had no choice but to return to the table at poolside. Maybe Zane was back. She fervently hoped so. She felt completely adrift right now and he was her only anchor.

Retracing her steps carefully, Whitney was just hurrying past the bank of elevators when the last car opened. She stopped, stunned, as she saw Zane stepping out.

Why had he gone upstairs?

He obviously hadn't seen her but was turning toward the rear of the hotel. He appeared intent on returning to the pool.

"Zane!"

Zane stopped and turned abruptly at the sound of his name. He'd been preoccupied with his phone call from Sheridan. The man had rubber-stamped his approach to the problem. Now if he could only feel he was doing the right thing...

His eyes widened. Whitney. What was she doing here? Reining in his exasperation, Zane had no choice but to wait until she caught up to him.

"What are you doing here?" she wanted to know.

Damn it, couldn't she ever stay put? "I could ask you the same question."

He was doing it again, avoiding answering her question. "I came looking for you," she told him. She looked at him accusingly. "You were supposed to be right back. That man makes me uneasy."

He hoped she hadn't inadvertently said anything to put Quinton off. He fell back into character. A part of him hated all this, but he had no choice. "That man can make us rich."

"How?" Zane still hadn't given her any details.

"I'm working on that," he answered vaguely.

Why were direct answers so difficult for him? Determined to get at least one, she pressed on. "Where did you go just now?"

She was acting more and more like herself, even if she didn't know it, he thought. It was the worst of all possible worlds.

"To answer the telephone. You were there when the bellman called me away." A thought occurred to him. He brushed her hair aside from the bump. Was it turning colors now? "Are you feeling worse?"

She pushed his hand away. This had nothing to do with her amnesia.

"No, I'm not feeling worse, but I am feeling confused as hell." What was going on here? She waved a hand toward the front of the hotel. "The desk clerk just said you didn't take any call."

He'd learned to think on his feet a long time ago. If he hadn't, he would have been dead by now. He wasn't about to tell her that he'd taken the call in Adams's quarters.

"Then he's mistaken. Maybe what he meant was that I didn't talk to anyone. And I didn't. When I got to the telephone, there was no one there." He shrugged casually, then hooked his arm through hers, gently ushering her away. "I guess they must have hung up."

She wanted to believe him—she really did. But she couldn't shake the feeling that she was missing something vital here. "Then why didn't you come back to the table?"

"I went up to our room." He saw Adams, the bellman who'd come to get him earlier, over by the bar. With a barely perceivable movement, Zane nodded to him. The latter looked relieved. "I realized that I left my wallet upstairs."

She frowned. Why was he deliberately lying to her?

"Your wallet? I saw you put your wallet in your pants this morning before we left for the hospital." She remembered seeing him pick it up from the bureau. But if she was right, what did that prove? That he lied about inconsequential things? Or was there something larger at stake?

Zane shook his head. There was pity in his eyes as he kissed her forehead. "You're confused, honey," he assured her. "My wallet was on the bureau when I came upstairs. Just where I left it. I had to get it. I can't have Quinton paying for the champagne."

That really didn't make any sense. "Why? He obviously likes playing the grand host. It goes along with the image he's trying to project."

Without knowing it, Whitney had hit the nail on the head. "Maybe, but you have to spend money to make money. Quinton expects me to pick up some of the tab. It's part of the game."

She wasn't interested in any games. She was interested in something making sense for a change. Nothing, since she'd opened up her eyes this morning, had. "What about what I expect?"

"I wasn't aware that you expected anything." Zane wanted her out of the way. And safe. He was still naive enough to hope for both. He should have known better. This was getting really difficult. But he'd made his decision and had to stick by it. Too much was at stake. "Do you want to go upstairs and lie down?"

"Is that an offer?"

Even as she asked, she knew it wasn't. He was like a different person when he was around Quinton—or talking about him. Just what sort of an attraction did that man hold for Zane? What was it she wasn't understanding here? Zane and Quinton didn't appear to have anything in common.

Zane shook his head. "It's a suggestion."

She sighed as they made their way through the crowd. It seemed to have swelled in the past half hour. "You mean alone, don't you?"

This really wasn't going to go down well once she recovered her memory. And he was going to play it for all he was worth. Maybe they'd both share a laugh over it. Eventually. Anticipation had him smiling despite his annoyance.

"How else can you get some rest?"

"I don't want rest, I'm restless." What was the use? Whitney waved her own words aside. "Never mind, let's just get this over with."

She made it sound as if she thought this was the last they were seeing of the other couple. But it was just the beginning. Payoff, if it came—and it had better—wouldn't be for at least another two to three days at the earliest, if he didn't miss his guess.

Zane lowered his voice as he inclined his head toward her. "I want you to be nice to Quinton. He could represent our future."

She didn't know him well enough not to draw the logical conclusion at his request. Anger froze in her breast. "Just how nice are we talking about?"

It took him less than a second to realize what she was asking.

"Not what you're thinking," he snapped before he could stop himself. Did she think she was married to a pimp? This was getting to be messy. "I just want you to be pleasant and smile at the man when he looks at you. I'll do the rest."

Whitney wasn't as easily convinced of that as she might have been earlier. "Unless you get another phone call."

There was no danger of that. "No more phone calls," Zane promised. He'd done what he needed to do. Now he had to be in Quinton's face until it was over.

He kept his arm around Whitney's shoulders as they approached Quinton's table. "Sorry." He addressed Quinton. "The call was unavoidable. Business."

Whitney stared at Zane as she took her seat. What was he talking about? He had just told her that there hadn't been anyone on the line. Why was he lying?

The look in Zane's eyes warned her not to contradict him.

Quinton took the explanation in stride. As Zane sat down, Quinton filled his glass for him. The bottle was close to empty again. It amazed Whitney that Quinton was showing absolutely no signs of being even mildly inebriated. What was the man made of?

Quinton eyed Zane. "What kind of business did you say you were in again, Russell?"

He hadn't said. He'd deliberately skated around the issue. A man didn't come right out and declare he was on the wrong side of the law, not unless he was an idiot.

And Zane knew that Quinton had no patience with idiots.

"Same as yours, Mr. Quinton." He took a sip of the champagne. Their eyes met in silence. Quinton understood him, Zane thought in satisfaction. "Investments. Land developing." Zane took another sip, pausing for emphasis. "A little of this, a little of that." He positioned his glass within the water ring it had formed on the frosted tabletop. "Wherever there's money, I'm there."

He didn't make it sound very solid, Whitney thought. And yet he could afford to give her a ring the size of Rhode Island. Business had to be good.

Quinton tilted his head, a raven watching a worm rise out of the earth, waiting to pounce. "Then why is it I've never heard you mentioned before?"

Zane laughed shortly. "People I deal with have better things to do than bandy names about." He waited a beat to give the next words emphasis. "But Werner's mentioned you to me on several occasions."

The name obviously meant something to Quinton, Whitney thought. She saw the dark brows rise, one higher than the other. "Hans Werner?"

Zane barely nodded, then smiled. "He'd said you'd remember. He told me he met you in Rio a couple of years ago." With hooded eyes, Zane watched Quinton's expression as he leisurely sipped his champagne. He was almost enjoying himself. "Said you were a very reasonable man to work with, once the terms were correct."

"I am." Quinton threw back his glass as if he were downing shooters instead of a glass of champagne that went for fifty dollars a bottle. His small eyes pinned Zane to his chair. "Where do you know him from?"

Zane deliberately played it cagey. "Like I said, I deal in the same commodities you do."

Whitney had the impression she was watching a very strange dance. For each step one man took, the other matched him, then moved one step on his own.

She glanced at Sally. The woman had tuned the conversation out and was amusing herself by watching a well-muscled man who couldn't have been more than twenty years old. He was strolling around the pool, blatantly showing off his body. The white thong he wore left little to be imagined.

The smile on Quinton's lips peeled back a fraction of an inch at a time as he regarded his tablemate. "Perhaps we can get together later and discuss this further, when we won't be boring the ladies."

Whitney knew better than to be taken in by the thoughtfulness Quinton seemed to be expressing. He just didn't want them around. For the first time, she wanted to stay.

"I'm not bored," she assured him with feeling. To prove her point, she wrapped her arms around Zane, her eyes on Quinton. "I want to know everything about my husband's line of work."

Quinton studied her, as if unable to decide whether she was the genuine article. "Sometimes, my dear, too much knowledge can be a bad thing."

"Ignorance is bliss?" she guessed, surprised she remembered the saying. "Only if you consciously choose it to be. I don't."

Quinton leaned over. "Take my advice. Choose it." And then he smiled as he leaned back in his chair. "Somebody as pretty as you shouldn't have to clutter up her head with details that don't concern her."

Was he for real? One look at Zane told her that Quinton meant exactly what he was saying. The veneer might be smooth, but beneath it, he had the soul of a Neanderthal. She didn't need her memory to see that. Whitney could practically see him dragging his knuckles on the ground.

Quinton shifted in his seat until he could reach into his back pocket for his wallet. He drew out a handful of hundred-dollar bills and tossed them carelessly down on the table.

"Sally, why don't you take Mrs. Russell shopping? Buy something pretty for tonight."

"Tonight?" Whitney echoed. She thought tonight would be private. She looked at Zane for an explanation.

Quinton answered instead. "Yes, as I said earlier, you two are my good-luck charms. I'd like to see if that luck holds up at the casino tonight."

Sally was already gathering the bills together and stuffing them into her purse. "You know," she murmured to him, "a credit card would be easier."

Quinton laughed. "Perhaps, but I like the feel of money in my hand." He looked at Zane, still trying to figure him out. "Nothing like the feel of crisp bills in your fingers, is there, Russell?"

Zane didn't want Whitney leaving, but there wasn't anything he could say without arousing suspicion. He was forced to nod his agreement.

"You won't get an argument from me. But you can save your money, Mr. Quinton. I can afford to dress my own wife."

To Whitney's astonishment, Zane handed her an equal number of bills. All hundreds.

Quinton liked what he saw. "I guess you can at that." He turned toward Sally. "Well, what are you waiting for? I asked you to leave."

Whitney could see that Sally didn't care to be ordered around, sent away like an inconvenience, but the woman rose. She half glanced at Whitney.

"C'mon…Whitney, is it?" She didn't bother looking at Whitney for an answer. "We're being dismissed."

Whitney picked up her purse. She could see that Zane wasn't happy about her leaving. The thought cheered her. Maybe there was hope, after all.

"Don't be gone long," he called after her.

Not, she thought, if she could help it.

Chapter 5

Sally, Whitney discovered, descended on the mall like a queen on a country she had already conquered. Moving from store to store with Whitney in her wake, Sally spent money as if it had been printed expressly for her use. The more expensive an item was, the better. It seemed to Whitney that she took a particular delight in spending Quinton's money.

The spree was a revelation to Whitney. She found that she didn't have much interest in clothes whose price tags could have easily been a down payment on a brand-new sedan. She liked her clothes simple but interesting. While Sally selected three gowns by a new designer who was all the rage and whose prices reflected it, Whitney's attention was drawn to an electric blue satin slip dress that looked as if it knew just where to hug a curve.

Easing it off the hanger, Whitney held it up against herself and looked at her reflection in the mirror, debating trying the dress on. So far, nothing had tempted her sufficiently to enter a dressing room. Sally glanced in her direction and surprised Whitney by nodding at the selection.

"That should make him sit up and beg."

Whitney hadn't expected a compliment. She ran her hand over the material. "You think?"

There was a smirk on Sally's lips. She turned her attention back to her own selections. "Trust me, honey. I know."

Whitney had no doubt that she did. Intrigued, she went to try the dress on. She was pleased to discover that the dress looked better on than she'd imagined. It *would* make Zane sit up and beg.

Satisfied, she handed the dress over to the closest saleswoman. "I'll take it." She saw a half smile grace Sally's lips. Maybe the woman wasn't so bad after all, Whitney mused.

The dress, plus matching shoes, were the only purchases Whitney made all afternoon. Sally, on the other hand, appeared to be determined to single-handedly resurrect the economy. They went to six other stores before Sally declared herself temporarily sated.

"Do you always shop like this?" Whitney asked her as the chauffeur-driven limousine brought them back to the hotel.

"Yes." There was no apology in the answer. "If I have to put up with Richard's roving eye, then he damn well is going to pay for it. If a woman doesn't look out for herself, no one else will. And if she doesn't look good," she said tapping the top of the stack of boxes, "no one's going to look, either." Sally looked pointedly at her. "I'd remember that if I were you."

"Which part?"

The spark Whitney had seen earlier in Sally was already waning. Sally stared out the window looking at Vegas by daylight. It wasn't nearly as impressive as it was once the sun was down. "Both."

Whitney detected a note of sadness in the woman's voice. She didn't envy her. The next moment, she found herself wondering if, perhaps, they were in the same boat. Beneath the trappings, were Zane and Quinton alike? Her first reaction was to say no.

Her second was to wonder.

By the time they returned to the hotel, Whitney had managed to place her insecurities about Zane on hold until she had more to go on. For now, she would proceed slowly.

The long, exhausting hours she had endured shopping with Sally were all worth it once she saw the look on Zane's face when she emerged from the bathroom in her new purchase.

Zane had spent the better part of the afternoon concerned about her. When she'd entered the suite, packages in her arms, he knew he'd worried needlessly. Instead of showing him what she'd bought, she'd disappeared with her packages into the bathroom. And remained there a long time.

He'd been just about to knock on the door to ask her to hurry up when the door suddenly opened. Surprised, Zane stepped back to let her pass.

The blue material glided seductively along her body like the softest of rose petals. Very sexy rose petals, Zane thought, almost against his will. His eyes skimmed over her outline. Unless he missed his guess, she wasn't wearing anything underneath. Not if the smooth, flowing lines were any indication.

Zane felt something tightening in his gut. And lower. "Wow," he whispered.

His reaction, not to mention the appreciative expression on his face, pleased her. She moved toward him very slowly, aware of the way the material brushed along her body. Like the gentle touch of a lover. She wondered if Zane would touch her that way.

She wanted to find out.

Her eyes held his. Whitney had her answer. "Then you like it?"

It was an effort to look up at her face. "I'd have to be dead not to like it."

"Good." Her body teasingly close to his, Whitney threaded her arms around his neck. The breeze from the window fluttered her dress along his skin. She saw desire flaring in his eyes.

Yes!

Whitney tilted her head, a silent offer whispering in her eyes. "Then pick up the telephone and tell Quinton that we'll take a rain check."

Zane didn't have to feign reluctance. He felt it in every fiber of his being. He fervently wished that the scenario had laid itself out in a different way. But it hadn't, and right now he wasn't at liberty to follow through with what his body was urgently begging him to do.

He would probably never be at liberty to, he thought with no small regret. Because if Whitney hadn't lost her memory, this wouldn't have been happening. She'd made their positions clear from the first.

Very carefully, with the sincerest of apologies on his face, Zane removed her arms from around his neck. "Can't do that."

So much for Sally's predictions. The man seemed to be made out of stone. Either that or she just wasn't being seductive enough. He seemed completely unmovable and unaffected.

Well, almost completely, Whitney amended with a pleased smile as she let her eyes drift down the length of his body.

Still, she was disappointed. Bitterly so. Things were not going the way she assumed they were meant to. She wanted him to sweep her into his arms, to crush her mouth to his and say the hell with the world beyond the door.

She wanted him to make her feel safe in this new world she found herself in. He was all she had to hang on to.

The ruffled shirt he'd put on was hanging open around his chest. Whitney lightly ran her fingertips over the downy hair, just barely touching it. She saw desire winking in and out of his eyes again.

Maybe all he needed was a little more encouragement. "I thought this was supposed to be our honeymoon."

He caught her hand in his. She was really getting to him. It had to be because he was so tense about what was going down, he rationalized, but that didn't change the way he was reacting to her.

"It is. But there's no harm in mixing business with pleasure."

So far, all she'd seen was the business side of it. She wanted the pleasure to begin. "I don't know about that." Resigned, Whitney turned and presented her back to him. "I need a little help with the zipper." She bit her lower lip, making one last attempt. "Up or down, it's your choice."

He sighed. She shivered as she felt his breath on her back.

Zane grasped the zipper's tongue between his thumb

and forefinger. With a tug, he pulled it up. "Up, and it's not my choice."

Whitney turned, smoothing out the material along her hips. She saw the way he watched her. Why wasn't he doing anything about it? "Then whose? I don't see anyone else in here with us."

But there was. There was the other Whitney, and she was hovering just on the outskirts. When she returned, there would be reckonings to make. And hell to pay.

Zane looked down into her face. "Whit, someday, when your memory comes back, you'll understand."

She thought of the telephone call he hadn't taken but told Quinton that he had and the wallet Zane had gone to fetch, which they both knew was in his back pocket the whole time. No, she didn't think that the return of her memory was going to make any sense out of that. Or out of a great many things that were giving her trouble.

Who was this man, really, who she was hoping was her compass out of the foggy region she found herself in? So far, he wasn't acting the part of a newlywed husband. Not unless there was something going on that she didn't understand.

She wasn't very hopeful about her condition, either, even though she was becoming accustomed to it. "I don't know if my memory's ever going to come back."

This part really wasn't like her, he thought. Whitney might be a realist, but under all that, she was a confirmed optimist. So much so that at times it made him crazy.

"Give it time, Whitney. It's only been less than a day."

He began buttoning his shirt again. It hadn't gotten any easier the second time around. His fingers were still too clumsy to handle the tiny pearl-like buttons and the holes they were supposed to fit through. Muttering a curse, he stopped fussing. When he raised his eyes, she was looking at him with the strangest expression. And he saw frustration. Genuine frustration.

His expression softened. This had to be really rough. "How are you holding up?"

She shrugged. One of the slender straps slid down her shoulder. Whitney pushed it back into place. "As well as can be expected, I guess." Her own words mocked her. "Although I don't know what's expected."

He felt so guilty. Guilty for her getting hurt in the first place, guilty for not telling her the truth. Guilty for the frustration he saw in her eyes.

"You're doing fine. Just go on being perfect." Knowing that Quinton expected him to come dressed to the teeth, he started fighting with the buttons again. There was still more than half a shirt left to go. "That's why I married you," he threw in for good measure.

"Is that the only reason?"

He knew what she wanted to hear. It was a small enough thing to give her, under the circumstances. He outlined a scenario, unconsciously elaborating on the truth. "That, and because I fell for you the first moment I saw you. There was a fire in your eyes that drew me in and took me prisoner without a single shot going off. Being with you seemed inevitable then."

Touched, she smiled at him. Whitney moved Zane's hands aside. Competently, she quickly slipped each button into its hole.

"You also come in handy," he told her as she finished the job.

She watched him comb his hair. Whitney stifled an urge to run her hands through it. "I thought that maybe you married me because I was good in bed."

The question caught him off guard. His eyes met hers in the mirror. "The best."

His reply was automatic. It was what he figured she'd want to hear. He had no way of knowing if she was or wasn't, but he had his suspicions.

Annoyed with himself, Zane banked down his thoughts. He didn't have time to let his mind wander like that. It was pointless, anyway. He'd made a decision not to cross that line almost from the beginning. No, he amended, *she* had made that decision for them.

Then they *had* made love before they'd gotten married, she thought. So why had he been so skittish when she'd entered the bathroom while he was taking a shower this morning? If they'd made love, she'd certainly seen him nude before. Try as she might, she couldn't make the pieces fit together.

He could feel her watching him. Thinking. Were things coming back to her? Or was she just wondering about them? If she remembered at the wrong time, if she slipped and said something to Quinton...

It was like sitting on a powder keg, smoking a cigarette and waiting for a spark to fall and set it off.

Whitney placed her hand on his arm. He turned and looked at her. "Show me," she urged quietly. "We've got a little time."

There had to be a medal for him in this when this was all over. A big one.

"No, we don't." Zane raised his arm to expose his watch and tapped the crystal. They were already running behind. "And besides, I don't think you should get yourself excited just yet. It might not be good for you."

She didn't want to get herself excited. That was his job. And just looking at him was doing it. That, and what he'd said to her. It had been the admission of a man in love.

Reining herself in, she sighed.

"No, shopping with Sally wasn't good for me," she corrected. "When she wasn't talking about clothes, jewelry or men, she was asking me questions. It was exhausting."

Zane raised a brow. "What kind of questions?"

"Questions about us, about you. I was deliberately vague because I couldn't give her any. She probably thought I was being coy. I think she has a thing for you."

"Just your imagination." He only hoped the answer was that simple. He'd seen the way Sally had looked at the men around the pool. And at him. He hadn't envied Whitney for what she had to go through. But it had been a fruitful afternoon for him. He was getting Quinton to trust him as much as the man was capable of trusting anyone.

Watching his reflection, he slipped the ends of a black tie beneath his collar and began to tie it. "So what men did you talk about?"

"I don't know any men," Whitney pointed out. Whatever men she'd known prior to this morning all resided in a murky world she had no access to. "She did all the talking." Whitney smiled. "I've got a feeling that she does more than that."

Zane smoothed down his collar. "Quinton better not catch her at it."

All hell would break loose if he did, she thought. Whitney laughed dryly. "If you ask me, they deserve each other."

Zane checked his wallet before slipping it into his

pocket. Ready, he crossed to the door. "No argument there."

Whitney was quick to get in front of him just as he reached for the doorknob. "Then why are we in such a rush to be there with them?"

He wanted her. There wasn't much she was sure of, but she was sure of that. And she certainly wanted him. It didn't make any sense to go downstairs when all the fireworks were in this room.

She was making this damn difficult for him. More difficult than she had any way of knowing. He combed his hand through her hair, cupping her cheek. Even the feel of it excited him. He was going to have to watch himself if he didn't want to trip himself up.

"It's not that I don't want to, Whitney. I can't. We can't."

Whitney read between the lines. "My health," she guessed, disgusted.

She nursed the hope that making love with Zane would trigger something that would turn everything around for her. That was healthy, wasn't it? Getting her mind back. And even if it didn't return in a mighty flash, she had a feeling that making love with Zane was an experience she definitely didn't want to miss.

"Your health," Zane agreed. He picked up her purse from the bed and held it out to her. "Come on, they're waiting."

Resigned, she took the small purse and slipped the delicate chain onto her shoulder.

"Atta girl." Relieved, Zane kissed the top of her head.

If she was going to get a consolation prize, he was going to have to do better than that. As Zane opened the door, she placed her hand on top of his. "Wait."

Now what? He looked at her expectantly.

"One for the road," she announced just before she kissed him.

And in case it was going to be a long, winding road, she put everything she had into it. Her mouth moved over his, offering a tantalizing sample of just what he was walking away from. And what was going to be waiting for him once they returned.

Caught up in the moment and the fire, Zane deepened the kiss.

He didn't have time for this. They had to get going.

It was a losing battle. He felt himself sinking.

His hands roamed the bare expanse of her back, molding her body beneath his palms. Arms tightening, he held her closer to him, closer than a whisper. Closer than a secret that couldn't be shared with anyone.

He held her until he knew that if he touched her even one moment longer, he wasn't going to make that elevator at all.

Regret bit down, taking a chunk out of him as he moved away from her. She'd completely sapped his strength.

"We'd better get going."

The smile on her face was nothing short of wicked. "I had the impression that we already were."

Her heart was pounding in her chest so hard that she was having trouble drawing a complete breath. She felt dizzier now than she had when she'd first woken up this morning.

He'd never seen her like this. Bawdy, willing, wicked. But then, she wasn't herself. He had to keep reminding himself of that. And he had to watch out for her and protect her until she was.

But who was going to protect him from her? And from himself?

"To the casino," he prompted.

This time, she laughed as he opened the door for her. "Are you always this single-minded?"

"Pretty much." Zane closed the door behind them.

She shook her head. "I might not remember any of the details, but it's like my body is on automatic pilot whenever I'm around you. You must be one hell of a lover for me to keep coming back for more like this."

He grinned as he guided her to the elevator. "So I've been told."

She turned and leaned against the wall as she looked up at him. "By the multitude of worshippers who came before me?"

He tried his best not to notice the way the material clung to her breasts and how firm they looked. Medal, hell—he was on his way to earning a Purple Heart. Zane pointed at the button.

"Just press for the elevator, will you?"

"Yes, sir," she teased, pushing the button.

There were deliberately no clocks in the casino. As people gambled, playing for Lady Luck's favor, time seemed to recede into a never-never land. Whitney had left her watch in the suite, but her body gauged that they had been down here for a fair amount of time. At least three hours, if not more.

A lifetime, she thought, glancing at Quinton.

In the beginning, it had been entertaining, rubbing elbows with an assortment of people who normally wouldn't have been found together. There was everything from wide-eyed innocents to faded, jaded people, old before their time because they'd tied their futures to the wrong dreams. Whitney saw blue-haired women playing the slot machines, stroking the handles as if they were intimate lovers, shrieking with absolute joy whenever the machine spat out a few coins.

There were people with the smell of hardened gamblers about them, staking sums at the turn of a card or the roll of the dice that took her breath away.

Quinton fell into the latter category. He insisted on keeping them near him throughout the evening, telling them to stand on his left. When he first mentioned it, Whitney had thought he was joking. He informed her that he never joked about gambling.

The more Quinton won—and he seemed to be working on a streak—the more he was convinced that he was right. They were his good-luck charms. As such, he instructed them to remain where they were.

Quinton's insistence was beginning to make her feel nervous, but Whitney could see that it didn't bother Zane. On the contrary, it seemed to please him.

The evening had begun with dice, then Quinton tried his hand at the card tables. Now he had settled in at the roulette wheel. He'd left the first two a winner and was determined to do the same with this game.

Whitney was beginning to feel restless. She was tired of standing around like a decoration, cheering Quinton on when her heart wasn't in it. She wanted to go to her suite, to be alone with Zane.

"If this keeps up, I think we're going to be dipped in gold and hanging off some giant bracelet by morning," she whispered to Zane.

He grinned and nodded in agreement. But he gave no indication that he wanted to leave. A fair crowd was gathered around the roulette table. They'd formed early in the evening, when Quinton's winning streak had begun and they had followed him from game to game, hangers-on who lived vicariously what they couldn't afford to experience firsthand.

Zane was tense, she thought. She sensed it, though there was nothing about his expression to indicate that he was. To the casual observer, he appeared to be almost unusually calm and laid-back.

But Whitney knew better. It was almost as if she could see beyond his nonchalant manner. Maybe they had a bond, she and Zane, that transcended vows and the ordinary. She rather liked the thought.

Sally, resplendent in one of the gowns she had bought that afternoon, was hanging on Quinton's arm like a silver amulet. Her carefully made up eyes grew huge each time the wheel was spun.

There was no way to beat the house in the long run. But with the resources available to him, Zane had done his best to come up with a system whose odds were good for making Quinton a winner in the short run.

Zane had advised him to play conservatively at first, working his way up from one to one bets. But safety had little appeal for Quinton. He was up to a corner bet, where the return, if he won, was eight to one.

His chip was covering seventeen through twenty-one. The ball landed on twenty.

"You won again!" Sally cried. Her eyes glowed as she watched the pile of chips multiply.

Quinton took a moment to bask in the crowd's excitement and adulation. Then with confidence, he pushed the newly swollen pile of chips forward to a split bet.

"Let it all ride."

The man behind the wheel looked dubious. If either of the two numbers Quinton chose came up, the five-thousand-dollar bet would swell to eighty-five thousand.

"I'm afraid I'm going to have to check with the casino manager." He motioned to the man at the next table. The latter nodded and went off in search of the manager.

Quinton rubbed his hands together as he looked at Zane. "So, what do you think of the good life, Russell?"

Zane looked around. Quinton was the center of attention. It wasn't a position that would have suited him, but Quinton loved it. "It has its advantages."

"That it does." Quinton flipped a chip to a woman who had been eyeing him with an open invitation for the past half hour. "Where have you two been all my life?" High on winning, Quinton passed a pile of chips to Whitney, who accepted them reluctantly. "I won't forget this, you know," he assured Zane.

Zane knew for certain that the man would definitely not forget if he lost this round. He hoped the theory Sheridan had passed on to him held up.

This was what he'd wanted, Whitney thought. To ingratiate himself with Quinton. She could see by Zane's expression that things were falling into place for him, although she was still uncertain exactly where that place was.

When she'd asked him earlier if he was hoping that Quinton would back him in some venture or share some knowledge with him, Zane had remained incredibly vague, as if he didn't think she would understand.

He'd treated her, she thought, like a wife in a stilted sitcom, and she hadn't liked it. It made her wonder if she'd somehow misrepresented herself to him in order to get him to propose. She didn't think she was the type who was content to be the "little woman," receding into the background, Moreover, she wouldn't have thought that Zane would have wanted her to be.

Every time she thought she understood him, he changed a little, like a kaleidoscope shifting the pieces to form another picture.

She supposed that some people spent a lifetime trying to get to know themselves, much less someone else. Why did she expect to understand Zane in less than twenty-four hours?

Still, it was hard to curb her impatience.

The assistant returned to the table and nodded. A murmur moved through the crowd like a wave. It subsided as the wheel suddenly came to life again.

The noise, so much a part of the casino, seemed to abate as the crowd held their breath. Whitney didn't watch the ball; she watched Zane's face. Everything seemed to be riding on this for him.

He really bought in to this good-luck-charm business, she realized. Almost as much as Quinton did. The thought disappointed her a little. She supposed she was building Zane up too much in her mind.

The wheel began to slow. The tiny black ball hopscotched from place to place, flirting with first one number, then another. Before the ride was quite through, it settled into the seven slot. Quinton's numbers were twenty-eight and twenty-nine.

She could feel the wall of disappointment rise.

And then, at the last moment, the ball seemed to hiccup, skim one slot and then come to rest on number twenty-nine.

"I won." Quinton turned and hugged Sally. "I won." It wasn't a cry of joy, merely a pleased announcement. An affirmation of his superior position.

A cheer undulated through the crowd behind Quinton. The man behind the wheel looked as if he had wilted as he took columns of chips and added them to Quinton's pile.

Quinton had the air of a man who had just begun to play. Zane knew a single number would be next. Thirty-five to one. The odds of winning were astronomical. It was time to quit.

"Maybe you'd better call it a night," Zane suggested.

Quinton debated. He liked the taste of being a winner and the games had loved him tonight. "Hell, I could go on playing for hours."

Zane had no doubt, but this was definitely pressing his luck. "Yeah, I know, but part of winning is knowing when to quit and I've got a gut feeling that maybe it's time to cash in the chips for tonight."

A waiter walked by. Quinton leaned back to pluck a glass from his tray. He raised it to toast Zane, and then Whitney.

"Well, then, here's to your gut, even if it does look nonexistent." Gray eyes slanted toward the woman who was still hanging on to his arm. He was feeling magnanimous. "I'm sure Sally's noticed that."

There was no question in Whitney's mind that he was right. She also had no doubt that Sally was, first and foremost, a survivor. She would put her health and longevity over her libido every time.

"I've only got eyes for you, Richard," the woman purred.

"Of course you do, my dear. For as long as I want you to." He watched as his chips were arranged in a container to facilitate being carried to the cashier. "Care to catch a show?" he asked Zane. "I could arrange for a private one, if you'd rather." One word from him would be all it would take to have the management empty the room. It was all part of the perks the hotel offered in order to keep Quinton loyal to the casino.

Zane draped his arm over Whitney's shoulders, pulling her to him. "It's tempting, but no. I think we'll just go to our suite. Whitney's kind of tired."

Whether a woman was willing to go along with what he wanted had never prominently figured in his own plans, but Quinton accepted the excuse.

"Of course. Russell," he called after him as Zane began to walk away, "why don't we get together tomorrow, same time, at the pool? I might be willing to listen to your proposition then."

It was what Zane wanted to hear. "We'll be there," he promised. Bidding the other couple good-night, he ushered Whitney toward the elevators.

She waited until they were out of the casino. "Proposition?"

He nodded. "I'll explain later."

Later was getting to be very full, she thought as the elevator doors opened to admit them.

Chapter 6

Whitney walked out of the bathroom, brushing her hair. Zane didn't like the pensive look on her face. He liked the nightgown she was wearing beneath her parted robe even less. Watching it move along her body like a silent invitation made it difficult to keep his mind on something other than the fact that his resolve to keep hands off was swiftly dissolving.

The nightgown was one of several that had been packed to perpetuate the illusion of the honeymoon, should their room be searched. But hadn't she packed any cotton nightgowns to sleep in? Where was the football jersey he knew she favored? Why wasn't she wearing that?

Because she thought they were on their honeymoon, that's why. Well, he wasn't. He was in hell.

Whitney placed her hairbrush on the bureau and studied Zane's reflection in the mirror. She had to ask. Something had been bothering her, interfering with the image of Zane that was beginning to emerge in her mind.

"Did you book this hotel because you knew Quinton would be staying here?"

If she thought that, did Quinton? Zane's expression was impassive as he turned down his side of the bed. He paid extraordinary attention to smoothing down the comforter, avoiding her eyes.

"No, how could I know something like that?" He'd had a feeling bedtime was going to be one hell of an all-round challenge for him, and it looked as if he was right. For more than one reason. "I already told you, we met because I saved his life. You were there."

Whitney nodded, parroting what he'd said this morning. "You pushed him out of the way when a car suddenly came barreling down a slope at the golf course."

There was suspicion darkening her eyes. Zane toyed with telling her the truth and then upbraided himself for weakening. Given the unpredictable state of her mind, it wasn't a good idea. Telling her the truth might just make matters worse. He couldn't risk that, no matter how much he wanted to tell her.

"Right."

He was her husband, Whitney thought. Why would he lie to her? How could she doubt him? And yet somehow his reassurance didn't feel right to her. She couldn't explain it any better than that.

The only thing that felt right was when he held her. Was she jeopardizing that by pressing this point? By making him feel that she didn't trust him?

Whitney shrugged, slipping off her robe. She let it drop at the foot of the bed. "It just seems awfully convenient, his being here."

He was having trouble listening. Zane's mouth turned

to dust. Though the robe was all but transparent, the added layer had helped preserve an illusion of mystery. There was no illusion left. Only a whisper of blue and the body of an incredibly beautiful woman beneath.

Damning the situation, he averted his eyes. With effort, he forced his mind back on the conversation and away from needs that were suddenly slamming against each other like a ten-car collision on Interstate 5.

He glanced over his shoulder, careful to look at her face and only her face. "Just what are you getting at?"

Helpless, she spread her hands. "I don't know. I just don't know."

She paced in front of the bed. The nightgown skimmed along his arm as she passed, making every fiber of his body tighten like a coil about to be released. Whitney swung around to face him.

"That's just it. I don't know anything." Whitney looked at him, unable to suppress the accusation in her voice. "And every time I turn around to ask, you're talking to Quinton." It didn't make sense. His behavior didn't make sense. One moment he was the concerned husband, the next minute he was a preoccupied so-called businessman. Which was the real Zane? "I need questions answered, Zane."

His voice was kind, sympathetic. "I know you do." But he wasn't going to be able to answer anything if she remained standing in front of him like this. He took her by the hand and urged her to sit down on the edge of the bed. Feeling like a man on a tightrope, he sat down beside her. "All right, what do you want to know?"

Everything. Who I am, who you are. What we're doing here and why your mind is some place else when I know your body wants to be with me.

Whitney banked down the riot of questions and sought

for order. She began with today. "Just why are you trying to get so friendly with Quinton? And don't," she warned, holding up her hand, "tell me it's business. I want to know what kind of business."

He was prepared for that. Quinton had a facade he presented to the world. A facade that included cultivating some very powerful friends, a few of whom were in high places in the government. Others that the government would have been afraid to touch.

"There's no big mystery, Whitney. Richard Quinton is a very rich man and has his finger in a lot of pies. Among his holdings, he has this property in Bedford Valley. It's at the very tip of southern Orange County in California," he added for clarity. "A huge piece of land, just ripe for developing." He watched her face to see if she was buying in to this. He was relieved that she appeared to be. "I want to go in on it with him. Manage the property for him. Set up a deal with a builder. Actually, I've got one already lined up. The designs are fantastic and the profit margin would be tremendous."

It sounded genuine enough. "Is that what you do?" With all the words that had been bandied about today, she still wasn't certain just what his actual line of work was. "You're a land developer?"

Zane nodded. He told her what he had told Quinton at the outset. Other things had quickly been understood. Bringing Hans Werner's name into the conversation had helped cinch it. "Among other things."

She'd had a feeling there was more. He was holding back something from her. "What other things?"

"I'm an entrepreneur." It was a description vague enough to cover and legitimize a variety of activities. It was the same one Quinton used. "Some might say an opportunist.'' And some had called him a hell of a lot of other things in his time. ''I harvest opportunities whenever I can. This land deal is particularly lucrative right now.'' Zane took her hand in his, careful not to look at her thigh where it had rested. He nodded at the rings she wore. ''So far, I guess you could say I've done rather well.''

She could feel her skin tingling. He was trying not to look at her. But he was. And his gaze was warm. Why was he playing these games? Why couldn't he just make love with her? ''Are you talking about me or the jewelry?''

He let her hand go and rose. He couldn't take sitting so close to her anymore. Not when he wanted nothing more than to crush her to him, to tear away that little bit of nothing she was wearing and lose himself in the scent and feel of her.

What he needed was a cold shower and a cold drink. Or, in absence of that, a hot woman.

But not her. No matter how much he wanted her.

''Both,'' he answered.

It didn't seem that way. Whitney regarded his back. It seemed almost rigid. She rose to join him. ''And what do I do?''

There was a full moon out. It hung on a canvas of black velvet. There were no stars. Zane made a wish, anyway. He wished himself anywhere but here. Without a star, the wish remained unfulfilled.

''What do you mean?'' he asked.

''With my life. What do I do when I'm not hitting my head and coming down with amnesia on my honeymoon?''

She was too close again. Casually, he moved back toward the bureau. ''You're my wife. You love me.''

Somehow that rang hollow. Especially after today's shopping trip. There had to be something else she did with herself.

"That's it?"

Zane smiled to himself. He was talking to the other Whitney now, even if she wasn't aware of it just yet. And the other Whitney would have cut off precious parts of his anatomy if she caught him staring at her like that. He knew that for certain. "Well, you've only had the position for a few days."

It still didn't sound right. "I have no career? No job?"

He fed her the bio he'd crafted. "You were an office manager at an insurance company." Because looking at her reflection was almost worst than seeing the real thing, he turned around. "You couldn't wait to get out."

Whitney listened to what he told her, yet it was like hearing about someone else's life. Hadn't she wanted to make something of herself, aspired to something? To be a doctor, a lawyer, a journalist? A fire fighter? Something, anything but a hothouse flower that had to be tended and nurtured?

He could almost see her processing his words. And guessed at the outcome. She might not know herself, but he did. And he had no doubts that consciously or unconsciously, none of this was resting well with her. Whitney liked to be in control of things, knowledgeable. Sitting back had never been her style.

"Does any of it sound familiar to you, Whit?" He knew it wouldn't, but it was the thing to ask right about now.

The troubled look in her eyes stung at a conscience he'd long since thought deadened. She was lost at sea and he couldn't throw her a lifeline without bringing other things into jeopardy.

He didn't delude himself into thinking that if he said the right word, everything would just pop back into place for her. That only happened in the movies. But what he was afraid of was that any stray piece of genuine information might put both of their lives into danger if she let the wrong thing slip at the wrong time.

A quaint saying played across his mind. Loose lips sink ships. Except that she wouldn't know hers were loose. He had to make sure that they weren't. Who would have thought he'd have to play guardian angel as well at this stage of the game?

Well, whatever he was, he was stuck playing two sides of a charade and hoped to God he could keep it all straight in his mind.

"No," she said slowly. "None of it sounds even vaguely familiar."

He refrained from taking her into his arms and comforting her. She looked like every man's fantasy come to life. "The doctor at the hospital said it would take time."

She remembered. She also remembered something else. "It could also be never."

Zane kept the length of the bed between them. "I don't believe that."

For a second, she'd allowed herself to get lost in an ocean of self-pity. Her head jerked up at the life preserver that was suddenly bobbing in the dark waters.

"You don't?"

Maybe if he told her the truth— But with enormous effort he kept silent. At least he could encourage her.

"No. You're a fighter." He looked into her eyes. "You're in there somewhere, Whitney, and you're going to come out swinging." She'd be swinging at *him*, all right, if she remembered all the lies he'd had to feed her. "Until then, you're just going to have to be patient."

She had to believe him. She had no choice. The alternative was too horrid. But she needed more to hang on to. "Tell me about the house."

"What house?"

Why was she constantly struck by the feeling that drawing information from Zane was like pulling teeth? Why was he so reluctant for her to remember her life with him? He should be volunteering things, not waiting for her to drag it out of him.

"Our house." Maybe she had jumped to a wrong conclusion. "We do have a house, don't we? I mean, I just assumed, with all the money you said you have, and being a land developer..."

Then she did believe him. That was good. "Yeah, we have a house."

He thought of the one he'd been taken from as a child. The one foster home where he'd wanted to remain. But the woman he would have willingly thought of as his mother had become ill, and social services had come for him, to take him back into the system. It had never been the same after that. There had been an up side, though. Being taken away like that had caused him to harden his heart and taught him a valuable lesson: nothing good lasted.

"It's a pretty place, two story. White stucco, blue wood trim." He grinned. "Not nearly as blue as that dress you wore tonight, but blue. Small rooms," he recalled. "Small house, actually, but it's got a good feel to it."

"Small?" Whitney echoed in surprise. From what she'd heard today, she would have thought that Zane would have picked something large and showy. She liked the fact that he hadn't.

He nodded. "Some things are best small."

Like small, firm breasts that were just large enough to fill a man's hand. And his night.

Damn, he was going to have to exercise better control than this over his mind. What the hell was wrong with him, anyway?

"Except for the bedroom," he continued, concentrating. This time, he became creative. "That's large. There's a sitting area, with a big-screen TV on one wall." Zane grinned, thinking of all the ballgames he could watch in a room like that. Sports were his one weakness. "I like being up on the latest technology in electronics," he told her. He didn't bother to add that at times that had saved his life.

A lovely, warm house. Had she seen it before? Was she happy there? Suddenly, Whitney wanted very much to see it.

"It sounds wonderful. Why don't we go there now?" Turning to look at him, she scrambled up to her knees on top of the bed. "Why not cut the honeymoon short and just go home?"

She wanted to get the feel of it, the feel of a place that would welcome her. Most of all, she wanted to be rid of this emptiness that haunted her no matter how much she tried to block it out.

"Soon, Whitney," Zane promised. "Soon."

She sighed, sitting down again. Her nightgown pooled around her like painted water. "Seems as if everything is on hold. Including us."

He knew it would come back to that. Because his own thoughts kept returning to the same thing. "I already told you, I don't think we should do anything yet."

Zane deliberately avoided using the term *making love.* Saying it aloud seemed too seductive somehow, and he was having enough trouble reining himself in as it was. All the discipline he'd exercised up to this point was wearing thin. The thing with discipline was that you had to practice it all the time. Otherwise, you lost control.

Her gaze slid along his torso. He was wearing pajama bottoms. She longed to run her hand along his flat belly. To touch him. "But it might help me remember."

No it wouldn't. But it would make for one hell of a memory. At least for him.

"And it might be traumatic," he contradicted. "I mean, I'm basically a stranger to you. Besides—" he brushed her bangs aside "—that bump on your head is still there."

A sexy, mischievous smile slid over her lips. "I promise I won't use my head."

He laughed. She was completely incorrigible. He wished she'd been like this before. Then maybe things would have been different. Hell, there was no maybe about it, they would have been.

But the fact was that they weren't and he was stuck with that. He couldn't take advantage of her no matter how his body yearned.

"Maybe you're not using your head, but I am."

Either he was the world's strongest man, or he had absolutely no sex drive. She couldn't believe the latter. Maybe there was a third reason. Maybe he just didn't find her attractive. Maybe there'd been another reason he'd married her besides love. One he wasn't telling her. "Don't you want me?"

He couldn't very well say that he didn't, not when they were on their honeymoon. Even if he lied and said he didn't, she had only to look into his eyes to know that he did.

His eyes held hers. "Whitney, I want you so much that it hurts inside. Believe me, this is a lot harder on me than it is on you."

She believed him. He thought he was being noble. Whitney sighed, defeated. Here she was in one of the most exciting cities in the country, in a gorgeous room wearing what amounted to blue cellophane, practically throwing herself at her husband and managing only to bounce off his muscles. And the walls.

"Don't bet on it."

"But I am." Leaning over, he pulled aside the cover on her side of the bed. "Now why don't you get some rest?"

Not waiting for an answer, he slid into his side. Zane turned his back to her and reached for the light, then switched it off. He could feel Whitney getting in beside him. In self-defense, he began to conjure up images of very cold places.

It didn't help.

"Zane?"

Her voice floated to him in the dark. Small, lost. Vulnerable. He felt his stomach tightening in response. "Yes?"

The dark made her feel needy. So needy that she didn't know if she could bear it. It wasn't in her nature to beg—that much she knew about herself. But somehow it didn't matter right now.

"Do you think it would hurt anything if you just held me for a while?"

The request sliced through him. Zane turned around. Silvery moonlight was streaming in through the window, revealing the expression on her face. It wrenched his heart.

"No, I don't think it would hurt anything," he said softly.

Shifting, he slipped his arm around her and held her close to him. With a sigh, Whitney rested her head on his chest. Her breath rippled along his bare chest.

Yeah, Purple Heart. Definitely. Maybe even two.

He was the source of every question that rang in her mind, every haunting doubt. Yet being here with him like this, with his arm protectively around her, made her feel safe.

Whitney curled her body into his and hung on to that sensation.

Within a few minutes, her breathing became rhythmic. He knew he could easily slip his arm away and get some sleep himself. God knew he needed it.

Zane remained just as he was, holding her.

Damn, that hurt.

Zane tried to stretch his arm. It felt as if rigor mortis had set in. Served him right for allowing guilt to dictate to him, he thought.

Behind him, he heard Whitney moving around in the bathroom. She'd risen before him. When he had woken up to find her gone, he'd thought the worst. But she was here. Her memory, however, still wasn't. It was the first thing he'd asked.

Zane sat up in bed, moving his shoulder to and fro, trying to restore circulation. At least it was his left arm, he thought, though there was small compensation in that.

Whitney walked out of the bathroom. Zane looked like an eagle, trying to rev up for takeoff. A majestic eagle, she thought with a warm smile.

"What's the matter?"

Not knowing if she had changed out of her nightgown yet, he didn't look in her direction. Instead he deliberately turned away.

"My arm's stiff."

That was because he'd held her all night, she thought. It had been nice, waking up in the morning to find his arm still around her. The fact that he'd held her like that, even when she was asleep, filled her with tenderness. It told her far more than his words had. Zane really did care about her.

"Here, let me," she urged.

Before he could tell her not to, she got up on the bed behind him. Scooting over on her knees, she began to knead his shoulders. He had knots the size of walnuts.

She wondered if persuading Quinton to allow him to be his partner was making Zane tense, or if there was some other reason for it. Leaning against him, Whitney squeezed harder, trying to work the knots out.

"Better?"

"Yeah."

He was lying. He was completely unaware of her hands on his shoulder or what they were accomplishing. All he could think of was the body that was pressed against his back. The body that was covered by something so flimsy that it looked as if it could be blown away with a sneeze. Her thighs were brushing against the small of his back as she worked.

Her thighs and…

Shifting, Zane caught her hands in his. "It's fine. Terrific. You can stop now. I feel like a brand-new man."

She saw the way he was looking at her. Her smile bloomed, filtering into every part of her.

"Funny, because I seem to be a brand-new woman."

She sat back, her eyes never leaving his. "What should we do about that?"

He didn't want to talk. He wanted to…

"Get dressed," he said abruptly, dropping her hands and getting out of bed. He tugged on the waist of his pajamas, pulling them up higher on his hips as he rose.

She was getting used to this, she thought, wondering if it was a bad sign. "You know, for a minute there, I thought you were going to kiss me."

"I was." To prove it and to close the subject, he brushed his lips against hers quickly—so quickly that it was as if he'd scarcely touched them at all.

At a loss, Whitney could only laugh. "In a hurry, are we?"

"Yes," he told her. "I am." Yanking open a drawer, Zane took out a sweatshirt and a matching pair of pants. The bathroom door slammed in his wake. He hurried into the clothes, emerging again within three minutes. "I've got to get down to the gym. I've already skipped my usual routine for too long."

It was a poor excuse at best, but if he didn't get out of here soon, away from her, he wasn't going to be responsible for his actions. Even saints had their breaking point.

Like now.

Whitney was lying across the bed, looking for all the world like heaven. And sin. The nightgown served only to make him want to unwrap what it didn't succeed in covering.

Whitney would have killed him for what he was thinking if she were herself. But then, he reasoned, if she were herself, she wouldn't have been lying there like that, tempting him.

Making his knees turn into butter.

He was weakening, she thought. "I've got another way for you to exercise."

Zane made one last attempt to make his rejection of her palatable. "We've already discussed that, Whitney. Look, this abstinence is hard on me, as well. But I don't want to take a chance on anything happening to you just because I couldn't control myself."

She rose from the bed slowly. Maybe he was right. It was just that she couldn't shake this feeling that she was finally free to love him and she couldn't do anything about it.

Her own thought echoed in her mind, surprising her. "Did I have a very strict upbringing?" Whitney asked suddenly.

He was almost out the door. The question, coming out of the blue, caught him off guard. "What?"

"Did I have a very strict upbringing?" she repeated. "I mean, was I hidden in a convent until I was twenty or told that my body would turn into a pillar of salt if I had sex?"

He began to laugh. What the hell was she talking about? "Not that I know of. Why?"

She shrugged helplessly. "I don't know. I've just got the oddest feeling about us." She raised her eyes to his face. "About you. That I'm free to make love with you and now, because of that accident, I can't. I thought maybe I was repressed and told that I wasn't supposed to have sex until I was married or something." It was the only thing that made even a little sense, although it sounded absurd when she said it aloud. "That maybe I believed that." And then she remembered what he had told her. "But you said we did have sex, right?"

He paused for a moment, trying to get the stories

straight in his mind. He was beginning to wish that he was the one who'd gotten amnesia.

"Yes. And you were fantastic." Because she looked as if she needed the reassurance, he crossed to her and kissed her cheek quickly. "And you will be again. Once I'm satisfied that you're all right."

And when would that be? She was afraid of the answer. "Zane, you're not going to wait until my memory returns, are you?"

She was impatient to make love with him. Who would have thought, he mused. "No, I promise. I just want to wait a couple of days to make sure that I don't add to what you've already suffered."

It was the best he could come up with and he knew it was lame even before he said it. But he needed those two days. And once they were over, he could explain things to her. And then she'd probably kill him.

He had to get going before he gave in. An hour of free weights and jogging should do it. Maybe two, he amended silently. "Now you stay put and I'll be back in forty-five minutes. An hour, tops." He was gone before she could answer.

Whitney frowned as she stared at the closed door. Frustrated, she got off the bed and went to take a shower. A particularly cold one.

Chapter 7

The small club was crowded with bodies and the sound of voices as people tried to outshout one another in order to be heard above the din. It was only if he listened intently that Zane could hear the music coming from the band in the far corner of the room. Around the band, people were dancing or simply moving in tune to another melody they heard.

Crowded, noisy, it wasn't the kind of place he would have thought that Quinton would be attracted to, but it had been the man's choice. After a second evening of gambling, Quinton had insisted that they cap the night by celebrating at the trendy club. Located at the extreme opposite end of the Zanadu, the Club Z was enjoying its own reputation as the in place, a place to see and be seen.

As if anyone could really see in this dim lighting, Zane thought. He looked around at the patrons elbowing one another out of the way in order to gain a small shred of space. There were a lot of customers here for what Quinton had to offer.

He could see that the same thought was in Quinton's mind. The man looked out on the floor like a wolf perusing a large flock of sheep, thinking about mealtime.

A waitress with jet black hair and dressed in sequined black from head to foot bumped against their table as she brought them more drinks. Murmuring an apology, she collected the empty glasses and distributed the new round. It didn't seem to matter who got what. Sally sat sipping hers, getting quietly drunk while Quinton tossed money around as if it was growing in his pocket.

He looked at Whitney. She was nodding in response to something Quinton was whispering in her ear, a smile on her lips.

An emotion Zane couldn't recognize began to cast out long vines around him, snaring a good hold. It had been three days since Whitney had lost her memory. Three days that he had been leading a double life. A triple one, actually, but who was counting?

He wasn't sure just how much longer he could keep this up.

Everything with Quinton was progressing at a painfully slow pace. But he could tell that the other man was beginning to trust him. As much as a man like Richard Quinton could trust anyone.

Despite his initial concern, Whitney gave him no reason to worry. She did her best to appear to be warming toward the other couple. To the outsider, it looked as if she actually liked them. Zane knew better and was grateful to her for keeping up a charade she didn't begin to appreciate or understand.

Given the circumstances they were laboring under, this was going far better than he'd hoped.

It was the other part that was giving him trouble.

The part that was happening when they were away from Quinton.

Whitney was systematically tearing through the fabric of everything he had managed to construct around himself since the first time he'd laid eyes on her. Tearing through it and bringing him solidly back to day one. Making him remember what he'd told himself he was going to forget.

Even now, thoughts of her, of wanting her, were creeping in where they had no place being. Where they couldn't be. He was supposed to remain alert, on his guard for any wrong movement, any indication that things were going awry. Everything depended on it.

And yet here he was, staring at Whitney, watching the way her mouth moved when she spoke, the way her eyes glinted at some joke Quinton had told her. The way her breasts rose and fell with each breath she took.

He hadn't noticed before how her hair was like a web of sunbeams trapped in a silken shower that fell about her shoulders. How her eyes looked like two perfect spheres of pristine pool water. And how her skin was like heavenly cream.

No, he hadn't noticed that before at all.

Or had he?

Yeah, he had. Noticed and learned how to suppress it. Successfully. Until now. She wasn't making it easy on him.

Damn, he was carrying on like some hormonal preteen about the latest nubile model to hit the magazine covers. He was a professional, for heaven's sake. What the hell was wrong with him?

Someone would have thought that *he* had been the one who had gotten amnesia. Maybe that was just the trouble. If she were acting like Whitney instead of this free-spirited, sensual woman, he wouldn't have to struggle to keep his mind on business. Whitney would have done it for him.

Zane looked across the small tabletop that was barely large enough to accommodate all four glasses. Quinton had been studying Whitney as if she were a piece of candy and he was a man with a sweet tooth that needed satisfying all night.

Zane blew out a breath as he shifted on the small chair. All that proved was that he wasn't the only one letting his mind drift tonight. But then that too was probably part of Quinton's facade: the successful businessman who had huge appetites to satisfy. Zane doubted that Quinton had to do any amount of great acting in that regard.

Given half a chance, he knew that Quinton would have taken Whitney away, intent on amusing himself. Zane felt more or less confident that the other Whitney would have been more than equal to handling the situation. But stripped of her memory?

This Whitney had no idea what was really going down. What was really at stake. He wasn't all that certain that she would be able to defend herself if it came down to that.

Quinton turned in his seat, placing a well-manicured hand on Whitney's shoulder. The gesture was far too proprietary to suit Zane.

"Would you mind terribly if I borrowed your wife, Russell?"

Yes, he minded. Minded more than he knew he should. Zane banked down the sudden rush of jealousy as he raised his voice to be heard. The band, in self-defense to the swelling noise, had begun to play louder.

"That all depends on how long and what for."

Quinton merely laughed. His expression made it very clear what he would have wanted to be doing with Whitney. Not waiting for an answer, he pushed back his chair and urged Whitney to her feet. "Is that distrust I hear in your voice, Russell? I sincerely hope not. That wouldn't be a becoming way to treat a new business associate."

Three days and evenings of dancing attendance. And six months of groundwork, not to mention two years of planning. It was cinched. He was in. Zane waited to savor the moment and found that the surge he usually experienced was muted.

"Then you…?"

Quinton inclined his head ambiguously. He enjoyed toying with people and Zane was no exception. He'd already placed a few significant calls and had the man checked out. So far, he appeared to be exactly what he claimed to be. That was no reason to give him any slack on the rope he was twisting on.

Quinton smiled to himself. The thing about being in the driver's seat was that you were the one who decided when to start the car and where to take it. He enjoyed the feeling. Exercised it every chance he got. There was no greater rush than power.

"Perhaps." He looked at Whitney. "It might all depend on just how well your wife dances." His hand closed over hers. "Ready?"

No, she wasn't ready. She wanted to leave. More than anything, she wanted to get away from these people. She'd tried her best, for Zane's sake, pretending that she was hanging on every one of Quinton's words, laughing at his stories. Humoring Sally. And all along, all she wanted to do was take a shower and wash the invisible film of dirt off her body.

But she wanted to make Zane happy, so Whitney acquiesced.

"Ready." One dance, only one dance, she promised herself. After that, if Zane wanted Quinton entertained, he was going to have to dance with the man himself.

"A man can't ask for more than for a woman who's ready." Quinton looked over his shoulder as he began to lead Whitney through the crowd to the tiny dance floor. "By the way, Sally dances only with me. Anyone else breaks her rhythm." The warning was stated mildly.

Sally followed Quinton's progress with eyes that were rimmed with anger. *The bastard.* She was getting tired of being taken for granted, of dancing on a string every time he pulled it. Of doing what she was told. She took another sip from her almost-empty glass. "Don't listen to him, I dance with anyone I want to." She looked at Zane expectantly.

If he was going to butt heads with Quinton, it certainly wasn't going to be over his mistress. "I'll just sit this one out," Zane answered. *And watch Whitney.*

Sally shrugged and wrapped her hands around the Scotch-and-soda glass. She glanced down at the bracelet on her wrist and then waved to the waitress for another drink.

Quinton had carved out a small space on the dance floor for himself and Whitney by using his elbow and the sheer presence of their bodies. There hardly seemed enough room for one, much less two. Quinton took advantage of that.

Revulsion filled Whitney. Quinton was pressed against her, using the crowded floor as an excuse. His feet never moved. But his body did.

She summoned a smile as she looked up at him. "Mr. Quinton, it's not a slow dance."

Amusement highlighted his eyes. He made no attempt to give her any room. Instead, he pressed his hand along the small of her back.

"It should be." Women were generally more willing than this one, once he showed an interest in them. He took it as his due. "You are a very beautiful woman, Mrs. Russell." As he said it, he pictured watching her slowly remove the green wraparound dress for him. He could feel his body reacting. "So, tell me, how is the honeymoon progressing?"

That wasn't any of his business. She curbed the impulse to tell him so. Zane wouldn't have wanted her to tell Quinton to back off. After a moment, she replied tersely, "Very well, thank you."

No, he didn't think so, Quinton thought. Despite all the kissing and hugging he'd witnessed, something was wrong between these two. She was too tense. Zane undoubtedly wasn't man enough for her. That could be easily remedied. Quinton raised a brow, ready to give her a shoulder to cry on. And a warm body in bed beside her. "Is he showing you a proper time?"

Defiance and loyalty had her raising her eyes to his. "Yes."

Perhaps, perhaps not. But Quinton was confident of one thing. He could show her a better one. "Should you, perhaps, want to have something to compare, I am at your disposal."

The pompous ass. "Thank you, but that won't be necessary."

"I wouldn't be so quick to dismiss possibilities, if I were you."

Quinton looked deep into her eyes. The laugh that rumbled from within his chest made her skin crawl.

"Just remember, during my stay here, my door's open to you anytime."

Whitney suppressed the urge to shove Quinton away from her. "Even if I were so inclined, wouldn't Sally have something to say about this?"

Quinton raised and lowered his shoulders as he turned her around in the small circle. "Sally has something to say about everything. If I listened to it all, I wouldn't have time for anything else." His eyes rested on the swell of her breasts. "Business or pleasure."

"I thought Sally was your pleasure." And right now, Whitney sincerely pitied the woman. Polish or no polish, the man was a monster.

Quinton laughed again, entertained. "I like you, Mrs. Russell." Then his eyes darkened just a little with a warning. "I would keep it that way if I were you."

Fear jabbed at her, stinging. Just what was he telling her?

Whitney looked toward the band. The drummer was laying down his sticks. "The music's stopped."

Quinton's hand tightened around hers. "I'm sure that it will begin again."

Was she going to have to dance with him all night if she didn't want to cause a scene? Relief washed over Whitney when she saw Zane approaching. Finally, the cavalry had arrived.

Zane laid a hand on Quinton's shoulder. "Mind if I cut in?"

Quinton released Whitney's hand. There was no room to step away, but he moved his body from hers. "There's no music," he informed Zane darkly. "You don't want to look like a fool, do you, Russell?"

Turning, Quinton moved people aside as he made his way back to the table. Zane slipped his arm around Whitney's shoulders. He couldn't put into words what he'd felt, watching them, watching Quinton hold her against his body.

"Are you all right?" he whispered against her ear. "You look a little pale."

Whitney didn't look at him. Now that she'd been rescued, her anger had an opportunity to boil over. "I always look a little pale when someone tries to maul me."

They reached the table, but rather than sit down, she picked up her purse. She wanted to be alone, to get some air that wasn't filled with the scent of smoke, alcohol and lust.

"I think I'll go upstairs to our room." She addressed her words to no one in particular. Right now she didn't trust herself to look at any one of them. The disgust and anger she felt might come spilling out. Most of all, she avoided looking at Zane. He'd been the one who'd put her in this position. "You can stay if you want to, Zane, but I'm very tired."

"Are you sure, Mrs. Russell? The evening is still very young," Quinton protested.

Whitney drew herself up. She spared Quinton a fleeting glance. "Maybe, but I'm accustomed to different hours. If you'll excuse me."

Without another word, she turned and walked away. The crowd swallowed her up within a moment.

Zane hesitated. He couldn't just let her go like that. What if she didn't return to the room? What if she went wandering off? She still didn't know who she was. Torn between what he wanted to do and what he needed to do, Zane made his choice. It didn't take him more than a moment.

Wallet in hand, he peeled off several bills. "Maybe I'd better call it a night, too." He tossed the money on the table. "Is brunch still on tomorrow?"

"Absolutely. I look forward to seeing you in my suite." Quinton pushed the bills back toward Zane. They remained on the table. "Well, what are you waiting for? Go after her. I wouldn't be wasting my time talking if I had a woman like that waiting for me upstairs. Go show her what you're made of." Laughing at some secret joke, Quinton waved Zane on his way.

With very little encouragement, Zane would have physically registered his contempt for the man. Quinton sorely needed that smile removed.

Later, Zane promised himself. Right now, he had some damage control to do. Heavy damage control, from the looks of it.

Zane took his leave. "Good night." His words were absorbed by the wall of noise.

Pushing people aside, he hurried to reach the door. Zane managed to finally catch up to Whitney just as the doors of the elevator car she was in were closing.

She was staring straight ahead and made no effort to push the button that would hold the doors ajar. Zane shoved his arm in and lowered it quickly, blocking the sensor lights. The silver doors opened again, then yawned closed.

Whitney continued staring at the triple row of buttons on the wall. "You could lose an arm like that."

She sounded as if she wouldn't have cared if his entire body had been sliced in half. Maybe he couldn't blame her. "All right, talk to me, Whitney. What's the matter?"

She couldn't believe he actually had the audacity to

ask. Her eyes were cold when she turned them on him. But they heated almost instantly.

"What's the matter?" she echoed. "You mean other than the fact that I'm on my honeymoon and my husband doesn't want to touch me? But he's willing to hand me over to a man he hopes is going to be his new business partner?"

The doors opened on the ninth floor. There were several people waiting to get on. Zane stood in the way, barring access as he jabbed the Close button.

"Sorry," he told them, "it's full." Zane turned to look at Whitney once the doors had closed again. "What the hell are you talking about?"

Playing the innocent didn't become him. And it wasn't convincing.

"You know damn well what I'm talking about. Offering a man your wife in exchange for favors." It was hard not to shiver when she thought about dancing with Quinton. "Quinton was trying to make an impression on me. With his body." The doors opened on twenty and she hurried out without a backward glance. "He's scum of the earth and he makes my skin crawl."

Her hand was shaking as she tried to open the door.

Very quietly, Zane took the card she was unsuccessfully trying to jam into the slot. Sliding it in, he turned the handle, then pushed the door open for her.

"Yeah. Mine too."

Did he expect her to believe that? She whirled on her heel, her eyes daring Zane to lie. "Then why are you throwing me at him?"

It had seemed that way, Zane realized. He'd asked her to be nice to Quinton, to look as if she was enjoying his company. How the hell else could she have interpreted his request? But he hadn't meant what she was saying.

He wouldn't have asked anyone to do that, least of all her.

Zane rubbed his face in frustration, at a loss how to make this right while his hands were still tied.

"I wasn't throwing you at him." Helpless and hating the feeling, he took hold of her arms and looked into her eyes. He had to make her believe him, even if he couldn't give her reasons. "Don't you know why I cut in? Because I couldn't stand to see him put his hands on you anymore."

The look on his face, more than his words, melted the anger she felt. "That's why you cut in? Because you were jealous?"

"That's why I cut in." Jealous. Maybe he was. "Look, Whitney, I don't expect you to understand, but I really need this deal to go through."

Maybe she would have been more forgiving if he could make her understand. If he trusted her with reasons she knew he was holding back. She had no knowledge of finances, but somehow, this seemed to be too much for just a simple land deal.

"Why, don't you have enough money?" She realized that she only had his word for the way things were. "Or is that a lie, too?"

His face was impassive but tension skewered him. Had she stumbled onto something? Had Quinton told her something while he was attempting to grind against her? "What do you mean 'too'?"

She pulled free of his arms. Three days ago, she wouldn't have believed that she'd want distance between them. But three days ago, she'd thought he loved her. Now she didn't know.

"A lot of things aren't adding up, Zane. Some of the

things you do, the things you tell Quinton.'' She looked at him accusingly. ''Us.''

He couldn't begin to explain things to her. But he was going to have to do something to partially clear the air. ''What about us?''

That's just it. What about us, Zane? What about us doesn't add up? The pieces aren't fitting.

''There's something dancing between us, Zane. Something tense, electric. Yet every time I reach out to you, you move away.'' She thought of the show they had put on during the past three days for Quinton's benefit. That was all she could call it—a show. Because once they were alone, the performance ended. ''You kiss me in public, make it look like we're two people in love, and yet when you're alone with me, when you could do something about it, you don't. You say all the right words, but your actions make a liar out of you.''

He shoved his hands into his pockets. He was being a liar, he thought, but it was against his will when it came to her.

''I told you—''

''Yes, and told me, and told me.'' And she was weary of the excuse, of the lie. ''I'm all right now. Except that I can't remember. It's been three days, Zane. Three days during which time I've been trying to figure out which end up is. And all I've been able to determine is that I want you and you don't want me.''

''That's not true. I want you. God help me, I want you more than I want to breathe.'' He shook his head. The words had erupted before he could hold them back. Before he could weigh them. He didn't want to feel this way, but he couldn't help himself. ''You're messing with my head, Whitney. I can't think straight.''

She almost believed him. Almost. "Makes two of us," she murmured.

There was anguish in his eyes when he looked at her. "But I can't...we can't..."

That was bull. If it wasn't, then he had to make her understand. She wanted desperately to understand. "Why? Why can't we?"

He grabbed her, wanting to shake sense into her, wanting to shake her until she was the old Whitney. Until her memory returned and she stopped torturing him like this.

"Because—"

His voice trailed off as he suddenly became aware of what he was doing. Zane dropped his hands. There were marks on her arms. From him. He'd held her too tightly.

"Because?" She whispered the word, her breath gliding along his skin. Whitney turned up her face to his, waiting.

And then he didn't know anything anymore. Didn't know anything except that if he didn't kiss her this moment, didn't have her, he was going to die right here, on the twentieth floor of the Zanadu Hotel. He'd never been so sure of anything in his life.

Struggling, angry, helpless, he surrendered. "I always said you were the most infuriating woman." Zane pulled her to him, his mouth covering hers.

Always.

It was a good word, a wonderful word. Whitney knew it would continue to ring in her mind long after all others had escaped.

Always.

She wanted nothing more than to always be with him. Like this, locked in an embrace, sealed in a kiss. Lost in the scent and taste of him.

Always.

His mouth slanted over hers, kissing her over and over again. Her head was beginning to spin, but not the way it had when she first woke up to find herself lost. She wasn't lost anymore. She was found. Whatever else she was to learn later would be secondary. She knew she had found herself and her soul, right here, with Zane.

Warning flags went up all through his body. He didn't heed them. He didn't have time. They were all disintegrating, burning up in the heat of the fire he felt coursing through his veins.

Zane ran his hands along her body, absorbing every curve, every sensation. Wanting her more than he wanted to live.

It might come down to that.

It wasn't right. He knew that. But right and wrong had been left outside the door, beggars who had to go looking elsewhere for their sustenance. All he knew was that he wanted her. Had wanted her from the very beginning.

And he was too weak not to take what she was offering.

Yes! Her body was singing as she felt his touch roughly possess her. Everywhere his palms passed ignited, sending the flame within her higher.

"Whitney." In a last-ditch effort, Zane struggled for the remaining bit of control he still had. "You're not well."

"Then cure me. Make me rise from the dead. I want you Zane. I have no memory. Give me something to remember. Be my first. And then you'll be my last."

He found the whispered promise irresistible. But Whitney wouldn't. Not once she knew. The ache within him grew.

"Whitney, you don't know what you're saying."

"Yes I do. I can feel it. I want you, and somehow I know that I've always wanted you. Don't make me beg. Leave me some pride."

Pride. He wouldn't be leaving her any pride if he took her; he'd be robbing her of it. And someday she would know that.

But someday was not now. Now there was only her, only this desire consuming him. And he couldn't stand up against it any longer.

With hands that were amazingly steady, he tugged at the sash at her waist. The material loosened around her body. Then, as he urged the straps from her shoulders, the dress floated from her, landing like a butterfly on the floor. With worshipful hands, he touched. Touched her the way he'd yearned to ever since she'd first kissed him.

And before.

She was wearing only the smallest scrap of silk. Her breasts were ripe and full. He almost swallowed his tongue.

"You're beautiful," he whispered.

He said it as if he'd never said the words before, looked at her as if he'd never seen her like this before. She knew it was only because she couldn't remember, but she cherished it nonetheless, grateful that she could store this feeling.

Heart hammering wildly against her rib cage, she lifted her arms to him.

Chapter 8

This wasn't supposed to be happening. The single thought beat in his brain like the last, dying strains of a song, refusing to melt away. He was supposed to be stronger than this.

And yet, if it weren't happening, if she somehow disappeared from the room right now, Zane knew he wouldn't have been able to bear it.

He moved toward her slowly, like a man walking along the ocean floor, even though there was an urgency in his eyes. Whitney held her breath, waiting for him to take her into his arms, waiting for the touch she'd been dreaming of the past two nights. And probably, she knew, for all of her life.

She looked completely vulnerable, soft. Stripped of the independent, flippant layer that he was accustomed to associating with her. He'd never thought of her as delicate before. But she was. Delicate and fragile and his to protect.

Look what a job he was doing. The reproach drummed through his brain.

But he had no defenses against this, against the need in her eyes, against the need he felt in his own body. In his soul. Doors were opening within him he could have sworn had been sealed shut forever. Doors that, once opened, couldn't be shut again.

He'd thought that he was incapable of feeling anything. He'd thought wrong.

Zane came forward. Came forward and met his destiny in her arms. Because, despite everything, this *was* Whitney.

There was no place else he would have been. *Could* have been. He no longer had a choice.

But he could give her one. Fair play demanded it, even now. Even if it tore him up into little shreds to offer. "You're going to be sorry."

He felt her breasts rise and fall as she formed the single word, rimmed in confusion. "Why?"

With superhuman restraint, he slowly combed his fingers through her hair, touching nothing else, though he sorely wanted to.

"You just are."

How? How could she be sorry when everything within her was crying out for this? When everything within her was moving toward him like the inevitable tide that longed to hug the shore?

"I'll never be sorry," Whitney swore vehemently. "Never."

There was a pull here far greater than anything she could have imagined. Far greater than her strength. Had she wanted to resist, she couldn't have. It was impossible.

He was her fate.

Her destiny.

She could *feel* it.

She could feel so many things. Her head fell back as his mouth roamed over her face, her throat, turning her body completely liquid.

And the liquid was near the boiling point. With a barely muted cry, she wound her arms around his neck, surrendering.

Zane could feel her excitement as it pulsed and transferred itself to him, urging him on. Fanning the flames of his own excitement.

He'd always sought control over every situation and certainly over himself. It humbled him to know that he had none now. He wasn't in control; he was being controlled. By his feelings, by a desire far greater than anything he'd ever encountered.

By her.

He was her prisoner. He'd never thought he would be taken prisoner so willingly.

Zane filled his hands with her hair, his fingers worshipping every strand. He cupped the back of her head and held her to him. For a moment, he did nothing but glory in feeling the way her body moved against his as she breathed. It seemed absurd that something so small should excite him, but it did. Everything about her excited him.

Kissing her again, he knew that he was completely hers. He lost himself in her lips, in the scent that surrounded her like an invisible cloud. He'd never surrendered before, never allowed the fiber of his being to slip through his fingers like this. It was scary. Scary and humbling and wonderful.

Zane raised his head and looked down into Whitney's face. Her lips were blurred with the imprint of his. He wondered if they matched his own. He could still feel her mouth on his.

"Do you have any idea what you do to me? Any idea at all?" he asked her.

It was nothing compared to what he did to her.

"Maybe," she ventured. From somewhere deep within, a mischievous glimmer surfaced, glinting in her eyes. "Why don't you show me?" she coaxed. "Show me that you want me."

Urgency drummed through his veins, throbbed in his loins.

He could have torn the last bit of material from her and taken her right there and then, shown her just how savagely his need for her beat in his breast. But that would be cheapening what he felt. What he wanted her to feel. When she remembered this charade, this evening, he wanted her to remember that this part of it, at least, was flawless.

That meant putting her needs far above his own.

From somewhere deep within, a single thread of control emerged. He grasped it like a drowning man grasped the only piece of driftwood within his reach and allowed it to guide him.

Zane slid his hands along her hips, slipping his fingers beneath the panties she wore. He watched the way her eyes widened, like sunflowers turning toward the source of their warmth.

Almost paradise. Just a step away. A breath away. He had but to pull his hand away quickly and she would be completely nude. Completely his.

Instead, his eyes watching hers, he slid the flimsy garment down her hips, a hint of an inch at a time, until it pooled about her bare feet.

Desire all but choked him as Whitney delicately stepped out of them.

And then she was his. Utterly and completely. For as long as there was a merciful God looking down on them, she was his. He wasn't very good at pretending, but he pretended that it would be forever.

Wrapped in his gaze, Whitney leaned forward, touching her cheek to his. He could feel her breath gliding along his skin, tantalizing him. Weakening him. Exciting him. Zane sucked in his breath as she nipped his earlobe between her teeth, lightly flicking her tongue along the edge.

If he ever thought himself strong, he knew better now. He was as weak as a kitten, hers to do what she would with.

Whitney grazed her palms along his body, glorying in the hard planes. He was magnificent. He was also fully clothed.

Her smiled teased him. "Aren't you a little over-dressed for the occasion?"

Without waiting for him to respond, Whitney began to work the buttons free. Her fingers fairly flew down the length of his torso, undressing him. Arousing him.

"I guess I am. You're the one with an innate sense of fashion. What should I be wearing?"

As he asked, as he spoke to her, Zane stroked her sides. He gently slid his palms along her waist and worked his way up to the swell of her breasts. She swayed as he teased them with just the lightest of touches.

Anticipation flowed through their veins in unison.

"Me," she whispered breathlessly. "You should be wearing me."

Her impatience mounting, Whitney pulled the sleeves

from his arms, sending the shirt to the floor on top of her dress and panties.

It took an effort to regulate her breathing as she undid his belt and tugged at the zipper on his trousers. She all but cried out in triumph when she saw the way he sucked in his breath as her fingers brushed over him in a silent promise.

Another moment and what little control he still had left in his possession would crack completely. Stopping her hand, Zane shucked his trousers and briefs off in one rapid movement.

They came together like two hands initiating thunderous applause. Like a clap of thunder. Violently, swiftly, to quell an irresistible need.

It was a wonder, he thought, they didn't set each other on fire.

But then, maybe they did.

The room whirled around with them, shrinking until there was no world outside themselves and this moment. No world at all to tell them that this was wrong and that the price of atonement might come dearly.

Below and outside were lights and noise and partying. Here the only sound was the wild beating of their own hearts, echoed in their ragged breathing.

He wanted to sample every part of her, to taste and commit to memory what, tomorrow, might never be his again. His mouth ravaged hers. She surprised him with the depth of her response, with her passion. By surrendering, she captured him.

He felt a prison door snap irrevocably shut. And didn't care.

Caught up in a storm, they tumbled to the bed, their bodies moving against each other's, vying for position, for ecstasy, already slick with anticipation.

He wanted all of her. And wanted to give her all of himself.

His mouth slid down along her breasts, lingering over each, delighting in the way she arched against him. As his moist tongue teased her nipples, her moan rang in his head like a mantra. Zane could feel her heart hammering against his lips. He felt dizzy with desire.

He'd never felt such power before. Never been so enthralled before. He was both master and slave to the same sensations. To the same woman.

With hands that eagerly sought eternal conquest, eternal knowledge, he caressed, cajoled, touched and possessed. And watched in fascination as she turned and twisted beneath his questing fingers.

He'd dreamed of this. Long ago and far away, he'd dreamed of this. But this was far better than any dream, any fantasy. For once, reality had exceeded his expectations.

Her breath was ragged, her body at once rigid and fluid as he did things to her she couldn't have ever begun to imagine. The sensations, the surprises, came without end.

It was as if she were a torch being lit and relit at his will. He had only to touch her, to stroke her, and she could feel herself hurtling over a summit. Spent, exhausted, she'd fall to earth, only to see the promise of another summit rising in the distance and find herself scrambling toward it.

Needing it more than she thought possible.

Desperately, she wanted to have Zane share in this wonder. She did what she could, moved by a silent voice. If she had any skills, they came naturally, because there was nothing for her to fall back on except instincts.

Whatever expertise she might have acquired before was all lost to her now.

She could only give him herself. And her heart. She had no way of knowing that was more than enough.

Biting her lower lip to keep from crying out, she drew his face back up to hers with shaky hands.

"I love you," she whispered a beat before she sealed her mouth to his.

"And I love you," he echoed, knowing she wanted to hear the words. Knowing that, at least for now, it was safe to say them. Because he could say he was pretending.

Oh, Whitney. I'm so sorry.

Arms around him, she reversed their positions. She was on top of him, moving along his hard contours as if every fiber of her body had a will of its own.

He groaned when she cupped him. The look that entered his eyes was one she would always remember, she promised herself. No matter what.

And all the while, as they discovered each other within themselves, an underlying feeling kept whispering through her.

Free.

She was free.

Finally free to give vent to this feeling. She couldn't understand where it came from or why it haunted her like a bittersweet melody. She only knew that it was there.

The freedom was overwhelming, bringing with it its own ecstasy.

Like liquid sunshine, she slid along his body, warming him, touching her mouth to his shoulder, to his chest, to his waist. As her mouth lowered, he caught her by the shoulders and dragged her up along the length of his body, smothering the groan.

Not yet, he thought. Not yet.

Without protest, she let him reverse their positions again. Within a blink of an eye, she was beneath him again, her body pinned by his.

Zane caught both her wrists in his hand, holding them above her head as he anointed her skin with soft kisses.

She whimpered, writhing, wanting the use of her hands to hold him to her. As she twisted and turned, it only served to heighten the excitement.

Exhaustion and anticipation divided her. And then she was refreshed, renewed. Eager to begin again.

When he finally slid into her, she wrapped her legs around him, wanting to keep him with her forever. Knowing that for now, this *was* forever.

The need for release was almost too powerful, but Zane fought it. Fought it for both their sakes. He wanted Whitney to remember that her pleasure was uppermost in his mind.

And then he began to move gently, a little at a time. She tightened and the rest was out of his hands. He moved more and more quickly as her body urged him on.

He heard her sob out his name as he spent himself into her.

It was over. And had begun.

Exhausted, he managed to gather her to him. A wave of exquisite tenderness washed over him. For as long as he could, he held on to the euphoria. But even now, it was turning into wisps of air.

Sighing, he began to shift his weight.

Her arms locked around him in protest. "No, don't move."

The sadness he heard in her voice surprised him. "I'm crushing you."

If he was crushing her, then this was the way she wanted to die. Her body pressed against his. "No, you're not."

The Whitney he knew was always more than ready to argue over everything. He was careful not to laugh at her.

"Whit, I'm too heavy." Then, before she could say anything else, he moved from her. But because Zane couldn't bear a separation just yet, he cradled her in his arms.

"I hadn't noticed." She sighed. Had she ever been this content before? It was hard to imagine that she could have been. There was just so much happiness a body could hold. "I think I died just then." She turned her face to his. "Did you know they used to call it dying when they made love?"

Where had that come from? She'd completely lost him. "Who did?"

"Poets. In those old poems." Long, winding epic poems written about love and lovers lost and found.

Zane stared at her, surprised. Alert. "How did you know that?"

His question echoed in her mind. A mind that didn't feel quite as empty as before. The words dripped from her lips. "I don't know."

Her memory was returning. Piecemeal, but it was returning. And with it, so would she. It was just a matter of time.

Why was there this incredible sadness when he thought of that?

He studied her expression. "What else do you remember?"

She didn't want to talk about what was in her mind, but what was on it. Him. Them. Lovemaking.

She moved her shoulder in a careless shrug. It brushed against him. "I don't know. A bunch of old movies or TV programs are knocking around inside my head."

He laughed, nodding. Yeah, she was coming back, all right. Wondering if he would soon have to say goodbye, he cupped her cheek tenderly. "You love that stuff."

"Then I guess it's all coming back to me. Slowly." She grinned in triumph. "See, I told you that your making love with me would jar my memory." She caught her tongue between her teeth, sheer wantonness reflected in her eyes. "Care to help a few more long-term memory cells make a comeback?"

He sighed as he brushed a strand of hair back from her forehead. "It's not a joke, Whitney," he told her softly. Only he knew how serious it really was.

She touched his cheek, caressing it. "No, it's not a joke. It's something wonderful. I feel as if I could leap tall buildings in a single bound. Fly…"

He'd never seen her like this and couldn't help the laugh that rose to his lips. "When you get to the bending-steel part, I'm leaving."

"Then I won't get to it."

She shifted, turning her body into his, reveling in the excitement that coursed through her.

He had no choice but to hold her. No choice in the world.

Her eyes were growing smoky again. Lightly, she rested her hand on his shoulder. "Is it always like this?"

He wondered if she would remember feeling this way when her memory returned. Or if the feelings that existed now would be superseded by anger and embarrassment.

"What?"

"Us. Is it always like this when we make love?"

Oh, if she only knew. He refused to allow remorse to color this for him. Not yet. Instead, he smiled into her face.

"No, this was better."

She'd had a feeling. She didn't know how she knew, but she'd had a feeling.

"Then I'm glad I lost my memory. That way, this makes it like the first time."

Testing the texture of it, she ran the tip of her finger along his lips. He closed them around it and lightly sucked. She could feel herself melting all over again, her body tingling. When he released it, she could feel herself tingling all over.

"The very first," she breathed. "I like that. It makes it special." She smiled ruefully. "I don't suppose I was your first."

Yes, he thought, she was. In a way she could never begin to understand. In a way he was having trouble with accepting. She was the first he'd ever truly cared about. And had, all along.

"If I said yes, would you believe me?"

"Sure." A grin played on her lips. "Why would you lie to me? You're my husband."

Guilt slammed into him with the punch of a heavy-weight contender.

"Right." To hide what he feared she might see in his eyes, Zane lowered his head and pressed a kiss to her shoulder.

Whitney propped herself up on her elbow, looking at him. Her hair was lightly brushing along his chest, tickling him. Tantalizing him.

How could a man who'd just made love get excited

over something as inconsequential as that? he wondered in awed disbelief. Yet he was. Excited and aroused. He found himself wanting her all over again. He would have thought that once he'd explored what there was, once he'd made love with her, the flame would die down and he could rein himself in.

No one was more surprised than he to find that just the opposite was true.

"So." Whitney drew small, concentric circles along his chest with the tip of her forefinger. "What do we do now?"

Zane pretended to mull over her question. "Well, it's a little late to go out again, but we could. Would you like to see a show?"

He kissed the hollow of her throat, setting off her pulse there. She shook her head in response to his question.

"How about getting something to eat?" The answer was a silent negative just as he adorned one breast with a kiss. "Movie?" He heard a stifled moan as he kissed her other breast. "Gambling?"

He slid his mouth down to her navel. She could barely turn down his suggestion as she twisted beneath his mouth. For good measure, he moved his tongue down just a fraction farther and heard her surprised intake of breath. He raised his head to look at her.

"Then what?"

With effort, her body taut like a chord about to be strummed, she urged him to her and then around, until she was on top of him again. Straddling him.

Like Lady Godiva atop her steed, the light streaming through her hair a pale contrast. Her eyes danced. "Guess."

He reached up and filled his hands with her breasts.

Her eyes had turned to smoky blue and he was captured within each orb.

"How many hints do I get?"

It was all the urging she needed. Slowly, she began to move her hips. She could feel his response beneath her. Triumph surged, indelibly stamping her.

"How's that?"

"Not bad." He could hardly nod his head. "I think I'm getting warmer."

Whitney grinned, inclining her head as she leaned over him. Her hair rained down along his body. He could feel his skin tightening, tingling.

"That's good, because I know I am." Her lids half closed, she watched him begin to stroke her thighs. The reaction was instantaneous, burning up her breath in its path.

"Warmer," she urged. "You're getting hot. Hot, burning."

"Can't have that. Can't have you burning up without me."

With a laugh, he flipped her over until she was flat on her back.

"You want hot?" he asked her. She nodded, laughter bubbling up in her throat. "All right, Whitney, I'll show you hot."

She was already arching up against him. "I'm counting on it."

Chapter 9

She woke up smiling. A soft, silken smile that poured through her body like fine, warmed brandy, reaching every extremity. If she concentrated, she could still feel him, the imprint of his sleek, hard body pressing against hers. She could have hugged herself, but she would have rather hugged Zane.

With a contented sigh, Whitney turned to look at him. Zane was still asleep. She'd almost been afraid that he wouldn't be here in the morning. That this had been a dream, after all.

She felt the desire to run her hand through the hair that fell into his face. She didn't want to wake him just yet.

Last night returned to her in glowing, vivid terms. Not just the passion, which was exquisite, but the gentleness, as well. The look in his eyes, which had told her more than his words ever could. Words could easily be lies.

But the truth would be there in his eyes, his beautiful green eyes.

The rosy glow within her grew.

Propping herself up on her elbow, Whitney was content just to lie here and watch him sleep. Tenderness filled her like a sweet song. It gave the contentment depth and substance.

Unable to resist, she extended her hand over his chest, keeping it steady. As his chest rose with each breath he took, it brushed against her fingertips. She could feel a tingle working its way along her body.

How she wanted him!

Hers, he was hers. What had she done in her life to get so lucky? She wished she knew what had attracted him to her in the first place. The worry nagged at her that she might never be that woman again, the one who had won his heart. The one she couldn't remember being.

Zane awoke with a start, catching her hand in a vise-like grip before his eyes were focused or even opened. "What the...?"

He groaned when he realized it was Whitney. Sighing, he released her hand. Zane scrubbed his own over his face. "Morning."

She wasn't sure if it was a greeting, a question or a protest. Just for a moment, she thought she saw something in his eyes she hadn't seen before. He'd become alert, from a dead sleep, like a man who was accustomed to being braced for the worst.

Why? Was there a dark side to this man who filled her with sunshine?

She was being paranoid again, she reminded herself. He'd just reacted with surprise, that's all. Whitney forced the smile back to her lips.

"You're awfully jumpy this morning." She curled her body against his. "I would have thought that after last night, you wouldn't have a tense bone in your body."

No, she'd just about liquefied him. He tried to get his bearings and erect a barrier against the guilt that was beginning to snake through his conscience.

He shrugged casually. "Force of habit. I usually sleep with one eye open."

And why was that? It was such an odd thing to say. Maybe he meant he was a light sleeper, she thought, searching for excuses.

Whitney leaned over and kissed him. He cupped her head, holding her to him. The kiss deepened, growing just wide enough for two.

She sighed when their lips parted. "They were both closed this morning. Your eyes," she added when he looked at her, puzzled.

Small wonder. Zane laughed. "That's because you tired me out."

She'd been the one who'd all but collapsed from exhaustion, not him. It was nice to know that some of it was mutual. She felt like a child with a new toy. "Did I? You seemed inexhaustible."

He'd always thought of himself that way. Until last night. But then, he'd never met a lover who'd been insatiable before.

"Just an illusion. All part of my charm," he confided.

And what other illusions were there? a nagging little voice asked before she could shut it away. With deliberate effort, Whitney disregarded it. "Now I know why I married you."

Her face was hardly an inch away from his. All he had to do was raise his head just a little to kiss her again.

Temptation began to take on enormous proportions. "Why?"

"Because you're an incredible lover."

His arms tightened around her as he lingered just a moment longer. "How would you know? You haven't got anything to compare me to. You can't remember." He studied her face, suddenly alert. But there was nothing in her eyes to tell him that things had changed in any way. "Or can you?"

She tried not to dwell on the frustration that had never been far from her.

"No, I can't." Her eyes were full of mischief. "But some things you just know without the benefit of experience. It's an absolute," she declared. Turning into him, she snaked her way up along his torso like a soldier inching his way up along the beach. "And you are absolutely wonderful."

He smiled at her but said nothing. It looked as if she was going to have to nudge him along a little, she thought. She didn't mind. The rewards made it worthwhile. "In case you're too sleepy to realize, that's an opening for you to leap in and show me just how incredible you can be in the morning."

He wished he was free to just enjoy her! "I'd love to."

She cocked her head, alerted by his tone. "I hear a 'but' here."

Amnesiac or not, she was always sharp enough to pick up on things. He dropped his hand to her posterior and gently stroked.

"Speaking of which, you'd better get yours out of bed. Quinton has finally invited us to his suite. For brunch at noon. We can't be late." Reluctantly, he withdrew from her and sat up.

But still, he couldn't quite force himself out of bed.

Whitney drew herself up, tucking the sheet around her. "Yes, we can. We can be fashionably late."

He looked around for his trousers. For a second, his mind was a blank. "I don't think he's the type to be impressed by that."

Whitney didn't want her mood spoiled, and thinking of Quinton would definitely spoil it.

"I really don't care what that man is impressed by." She placed her hand on his arm, silently imploring him to change his mind. "Zane, I've given it my best shot." She really had, but now it was time to think of herself, of them. "I've been nice to him, laughed at his stories, danced with him. I think that I've rendered service over and above the call of duty—"

He knew where this was leading and wouldn't allow her to go there. He had to change her mind. Quinton was superstitious enough to scotch the deal if he felt something out of kilter. Beneath the sophisticated image of an urbane captain of industry was a man who didn't believe in spilling salt, who hated black cats and avoided the color orange like the plague.

"Yes, you have and you've been wonderful about it." Zane wasn't accustomed to giving her pep talks. If anything, Whitney was usually the one pulling at the bit to get going. Shifting, Zane gathered her into his arms and lightly brushed his lips over hers. "But I need you to be polite to him just a little longer. He's almost ready to strike the deal." He saw the wariness in her eyes and knew she was thinking of last night at the club. "Stay at my side. I won't let him touch you again." He looked at her solemnly. "I promise."

She believed him and was torn. She sensed that there was an independent streak within her, yet it was nice hearing that he wanted to protect her. Maybe there was still a place for chivalry in the world.

"I can take care of myself. It's not that, it's just—"

"What?" he prodded gently, wanting to understand.

Maybe he was making a mistake, encouraging her to follow her thoughts to their end. On the one hand, it would make the operation easier if her memory did return. But on the other, how would he ever explain to her about last night? There'd be no working with her after what happened. It was better this way, keeping her completely in the dark for another two days. That was all he figured he needed—just two more days.

She shrugged. Maybe this sounded too self-centered. "I thought that after last night, things would be different."

They are. Trust me, they are. In ways you can't begin to imagine right now. But you will, God help me, you will.

"Nothing's different," he said lightly. "You're always terrific in bed."

She liked hearing that, but she wasn't digging for compliments. She was desperately trying to find the pieces of her former life, to become acquainted with them and construct a whole.

"Am I?"

He pointed toward his eyebrows. "See?"

Her own brows drew together in confusion. "See? What am I supposed to see?"

Zane's expression was totally innocent. "The singe marks. You nearly burned them off last night. Matter of fact," he said glancing down at the bed, "I'm surprised the sheets aren't scorched."

"We could try again." The words dripped from her lips, honey tempting a hungry bear with a proven sweet tooth. Whitney sat back on her legs. The sheet she'd tucked around herself drifted away from her breasts, settling tentatively about her hips. Waiting for him to brush it aside.

She tantalized him with each breath she took. He couldn't draw his eyes away from her breasts. The shower, her clothes and his obligations were getting further and further away.

He was lost and he knew it.

"Ah, now, what did you want to go and do that for, Whit?" Like a man whose free will had been drained from him, Zane gathered Whitney into his arms again.

"I would think that would be pretty self-evident right about now," she assured him. Leaning forward, she lightly traced the outline of his lips with just the tip of her tongue.

He could feel himself tightening, coiling. Readying for release. "You've got a one-track mind, woman."

She grinned, kissing the side of his throat. She felt his Adam's apple move in response, heard his breath growing short. "Better than no track at all."

He didn't know about that. Whitney was going to be one hell of an angry woman once she remembered. He only prayed he'd be lucky and she wouldn't remember this soon.

No, he amended, it wouldn't matter if she didn't remember. He was going to have to tell her once this went down. Nothing else would be fair.

And in order for it to go down, he reminded himself, he had to keep a clear head. That wasn't going to happen if he continued to allow her to keep clouding up his mind like this.

"Whitney, we really have to get going," he protested. But for a man who had to leave, he certainly wasn't making any attempt to get out of bed, he thought in disgust.

"One for the road," she coaxed. Lying back on the bed, she brought him down with her. He didn't struggle to get away.

"We're taking an elevator," he pointed out. Whitney could strip him of all good intentions without even trying.

She had him, she thought, looking into his eyes. It only seemed fair, because he had her. Right in the palm of his hand.

"All right then, let's make it one for the elevator."

He laughed, unable to resist her any longer. Not really wanting to. "You are one incorrigible lady, Whitney Bradshaw."

"Russell," she corrected. "Whitney Bradshaw Russell. You forgot we're married."

That had been a slip. But she made him forget everything but her.

"Not for a minute," he lied.

"And that's insatiable, not incorrigible," she pointed out. Whitney's smile spread across her lips slowly, as if daring his mouth to follow.

"Yeah, that, too." Who was he kidding? He wasn't going anywhere. Not right now. Zane glanced at the digital clock on the nightstand. "I guess we've got a few minutes."

Hands on his face, she brought it around so that his eyes looked into hers. "Good, then we've got forever," she whispered seductively.

It was happening all over again, that need for her, that feeling that if he didn't have her, nothing else meant a damn. Like a man possessed, he kissed her over and over again, branding her with his mouth, with his desire.

"Whit?"

How was it possible for her limbs to at once feel deadened and lighter than air? "Mmm?"

This was important, to him if not to her. Zane whispered the words against her ear. "I want you to remember that you started this. Later, I want you to remember."

He sounded so serious that she wanted to ask him what was wrong. But she didn't. Because he wouldn't tell her. She knew that already. All she could do was reassure him.

"I don't plan to forget any time soon," she promised. His words fresh in her mind, her gaze swept over his face. "I can't understand why, if I can remember Jimmy Stewart, how I can forget making love with you. You would have thought I'd remember something so memorable." She laughed quietly to herself, her eyes already making love to him. "I guess there's no way to understand."

"No way," he echoed.

And then there was no time for talking anymore, only feeling. Only touching and re-exploring places already conquered.

He took her places she already knew, but he showed her a new path there. This time, the lovemaking was frantic, explosive.

It was as if they were both aware of the minutes that were ticking away. Hers were minutes of the hour, tied to a schedule. His marked forever. He knew he was on borrowed time.

Zane took what was being so willingly offered, reveled in what he already knew. She heated beneath his hand almost instantly and he raced against time, against himself, for just one more taste, one more sample.

There might never be another chance.

His mouth touched her everywhere, loving the different flavors, trying to commit them all to memory against the day when she would remember. Or, barring that, against the day he would have to tell her the truth.

She was a feast for his body and his soul.

A feast he couldn't sate himself with. The more he had, the more he wanted.

Better that he hadn't known at all what loving her could be like.

But it was past time for that.

With skillful hands and an even more skillful mouth, he brought her up and over crest after crest, watching Whitney's face, feeling the final burst of ecstasy each time she did.

And then, when he couldn't hold himself back any longer, when their time together was almost gone, he sheathed himself in her and loved her one more time.

Last night, time and again, he'd been a gentle lover. In the light of day, he was almost a savage one. But even in the heart of this fury, there was a tenderness. It caught her by surprise and brought tears to her eyes. Tears of happiness.

Exhausted, she lay beside him. With considerable effort, she turned her head toward him. "Wow, what was that all about?"

He was wondering about that himself. He'd been almost unrecognizable to himself. Was there an antidote for what he was feeling? "Quality time accelerated."

That was one way to put it. She sighed and even that took effort.

"You know, I said earlier that I didn't want to go to Quinton's suite. Now I'm not sure if I can." She tried to prop herself up on her elbows and failed. Lips pressed together, she looked down the length of the bed at her feet. "I think I forgot how to walk."

He laughed, shifting so that he was over her again. He saw fresh desire beginning in her eyes. Obviously she wasn't as tired as she thought she was.

"Then I'll just have to carry you." He teased her with a quick, openmouthed kiss against her navel before sitting up. "Quinton wants a matched set, we give him a matched set." He saw the doubt creep into her eyes. "Don't worry, it'll all be worth it in the long run. And I'll make it up to you tonight."

And probably for the rest of my life.

He was making it tempting. She weighed her alternatives and began to weaken. "I can't stay here?"

If she had a cold, he would have left her behind with chicken soup, room service and a gun beneath her pillow. But she didn't have a cold. She had amnesia and was in more danger than she realized.

"I don't want to leave you alone. You still can't remember anything but the television set."

He was sweet. He tried to put up a front, but she knew better now. Whitney touched his cheek lovingly. "Oh, I think I'm starting to remember a few things."

Like what? "Oh?" he asked guardedly.

She nodded. "Like last night. Like loving you." She sighed. There was no putting off the inevitable, and she knew she couldn't say no to Zane, not if it meant so much to him. Digging her fists into the bed on either side of her, Whitney rose. "All right, if I have to go, I have to go. Just give me a few minutes to take a shower and get ready."

Not bothering to pick up her robe, she walked out of the room regally. And completely nude.

Even after everything, she still managed to overwhelm him.

"And I've got to remember to keep my eyes in my head," Zane muttered to himself.

Grabbing the trousers he'd discarded last night, Zane pulled them on and then reached for the telephone. He paused, listening.

The muted sound of running water reassured him. Whitney was taking her shower. That gave him approximately ten minutes, if she ran true to form. He only needed two or three.

Quickly, he tapped out a number. The call was being placed to an answering machine. An answering machine that sat in a Spartan office overlooking the ocean in Newport Beach. The number was his own, as was the office. It was a front. Both he and Quinton knew that and each knew that the other knew, but it was a necessary part of the charade.

If Quinton checked the list of telephone numbers printed out on Zane's account, it would look as if he was calling to see if he'd received any messages. They wouldn't assume that he was calling to leave one of his own.

Sheridan would have the message within five minutes.

The pick up came on the third ring. Zane spoke quickly.

"Hi, it's me. Whitney still doesn't remember anything. So far, things are going well." That depended, he knew, on which side of the bed he was standing on. "Quinton looks like he's going to bite sometime today, if we're lucky. His woman isn't quite the bimbo we thought she was. She's been pumping Whit with questions. Thank God Whit knows only what I've told her.

There's still a chance her condition might snag the operation, but I'm sticking close to her. Talk to you later.''

Zane replaced the receiver in its cradle. He nearly dropped the telephone when he saw her standing in the doorway, a thoughtful frown on her lips, beads of water sliding down her slick body.

Impulse had made her jump out of the shower, dripping wet, with the intention of pulling Zane in with her. The urge faded instantly as she had caught his final words. He was talking to someone about her. Someone, judging by his surprised expression, he hadn't wanted her to know about.

She felt cold suddenly. In defiance, she raised her chin. "Who was that?"

Mind racing, Zane slowly replaced the telephone on the night stand. "What?"

She grabbed a towel and wrapped it around herself. She couldn't quite explain or put it into words, but she felt violated.

"Don't play games with me, Zane. Who was on the telephone? And why is my 'condition' a possible problem to the operation? What sort of an operation are you talking about, anyway?"

Question after question was erupting in her brain, taking with it her recent euphoria.

When under attack, advance, don't retreat, Zane thought. *It confuses the hell out of the enemy.* It was a trick someone had once taught him. Whitney wasn't the enemy, but the advice still held true.

He didn't answer her questions; instead, he asked one of his own. "What are you doing out of the shower?"

"I was going to invite you in." It seemed silly now. "Don't change the subject," she warned.

Zane summoned all the charm he had at his disposal.

"There isn't a subject," he assured her as he slipped his arm around her shoulders. "I was talking to your doctor. I just remembered that you were supposed to go in for some minor surgery when we got back. I don't think, with this amnesia, you should go through with it. I was just leaving a message to that effect on his answering machine."

She'd only walked in on his final words, but she was still unconvinced. "Doctors have answering services, not machines."

"This one has a machine," Zane assured her. "I called his home number. He's an old friend. A plastic surgeon."

"What was I having done?"

"I don't know. You wouldn't tell me. Even after I said I didn't want you changing anything about yourself."

She supposed that it could be true and all very innocent, but she'd had the oddest feeling when she'd walked in on him. A feeling of déjà vu. And a feeling that things weren't quite right.

Whitney looked at him dubiously. "Zane, I want to believe you—"

He unknotted the towel. It began to fall and she made a grab for it, but he stayed her hand. The towel fell to the floor. "Then what's the problem?"

She could feel pulses beginning to throb again. "The problem is that I feel there's something you're not telling me. That you're keeping me in the dark for some reason."

He tried to look the part of the concerned husband and found that it wasn't a stretch for him. Maybe he wasn't a husband, but he was damn well concerned about her.

"Whit, you've had a shock. Amnesia isn't just a sinus headache. Some part of your brain has shut down, blocked things out. I don't want to burden you with too much information at one time. Too many things thrown at you at once might scramble everything for you."

"Scramble?" she echoed. What was he getting at? He hadn't given her too much information. He'd hardly given her any at all.

The shrug was born of impatience. "Yes, scramble. Hell, I'm just a layman. I don't know what another shock to your system would do."

He was still confusing her. She wondered if he was doing it on purpose. "What kind of shock?"

He could still hear the water running in the shower. Taking her hand, he started to usher her into the bathroom. "Did you come out here to play twenty questions, or to drag me back to the shower? We're wasting water, standing out here and talking."

She knew she should insist on remaining here and getting things cleared up. But she didn't do her best thinking nude. She began to smile as she allowed him to lead her to the shower stall.

"Is there a drought?"

"There will be if we don't turn off that water soon." He opened the stall door and glanced inside. "You know, it does look big enough for two."

"I think that was the general idea. After all, it is the honeymoon suite."

Zane closed the door behind them. Water cascaded over both their bodies as they jockeyed for position.

Whitney could feel herself heating again, forgetting everything but this man with her and what he could do to her with the slightest touch. But she needed to ask. To know. "Zane, *are* you keeping anything from me?"

The sexiest smile she'd ever seen crossed his lips. "Not for long in these tight quarters. It's deceptive looking from the outside. There isn't much room in here." He encircled her with his arms. "There's only room for one and a half people. I think we need to conserve space. What do you think?"

It was a ploy, all a ploy to make her stop asking questions. And it was working. "I think you're not going to give me an answer."

"Nope. I'm going to show you instead."

Zane kissed her before she could say anything else.

Chapter 10

"I don't think we're in Kansas anymore, Toto," Whitney murmured to Zane in awe as she looked at the two-story structure that had been added to the hotel.

Its architecture was the same as the central structure's and it was attached to the hotel by a covered breezeway, but for all intents and purposes the building that Quinton was occupying during his stay at Zanadu was a separate one. It mirrored the way she was sure Quinton saw himself. Distinctly separated from the crowd.

"How many more movies are rattling around in that head of yours?" It seemed uncanny to Zane that Whitney still hadn't remembered anything about who she was, but her brain continued to be a walking encyclopedia of old Hollywood films.

"I don't know, I haven't taken inventory yet," she murmured.

Whitney shook her head, bemused. At the entrance to Quinton's accommodations stood two tall, very able-bodied guards. Although one was burlier than the other, they had on the same harem attire worn by the rest of the staff at the hotel. They both looked a little oafish, but she sincerely doubted anyone would ever have enough courage to tell either of them that.

She thought of their bridal suite. Up until now, it had seemed rather impressive. But Quinton's quarters, even on the outside, represented an entirely different world.

"Are you sure that this is part of the same hotel?" she whispered to Zane.

Zane gave their names to the two men and waited as the names were verified against a list. "Makes you see why Quinton keeps returning here."

"Returning?" The guard rapped twice on the door and it was opened by a butler in full formal attire, down to his immaculate white gloves. Whitney had to make a conscious effort not to stare. "If I were staying in a place like this, they'd have to use dynamite to get me out."

Standing in the foyer, she looked slowly around, vaguely aware of the door shutting behind them. There was a sunken living room decorated with antique furniture that undoubtedly cost the hotel a fortune. In the very center of the room, accenting the cathedral ceiling, was a fountain. Aphrodite continuously poured water into a large seashell. It took Whitney's breath away. In the background was a winding, gilded staircase that undoubtedly led to the bedrooms. Her head began to spin.

She glanced at Zane. Whatever he thought of the accommodations, it wasn't evident in his face. "There are probably towns smaller than this," she said.

"Maybe," Zane agreed. "In Montana." He inclined his head next to her ear. "Quinton mentioned that it's sixty-one hundred square feet."

"Sixty-one hundred square feet?" Opulence had obviously been the watchword when the rooms were decorated. What could one man possibly want with a suite large enough to hold a convention in?

A noise behind them had Whitney swinging around. Lucifer materializing in a puff of smoke, she thought, watching Quinton walk toward them. Sally, like a well-groomed shadow, entered the room behind him.

Quinton's smile was wide and, as always, charming. But it wore a little thin to Whitney in the face of this overdone elegance. She couldn't help thinking that the money could be better spent by all concerned.

He took her hand in both of his, clasping it warmly as if they were old friends. "Ah, you've found your way to my humble quarters." His eyes on hers, Quinton nodded a vague greeting at Zane.

In a move he knew was far too territorial, but one he couldn't prevent, Zane slipped his arm around Whitney's shoulders.

"This is certainly quite a place." Zane knew Quinton would have been disappointed if he hadn't been duly impressed.

"Humble?" Whitney laughed at the irony of the word. "In comparison to what? The Taj Mahal?"

Her comment pleased him. Quinton's smile grew. After a moment, he released her hand and led the way into the living room. A living room that had been decorated according to his exact specifications. This suite was kept in reserve expressly for his visits. He wouldn't have occupied it if he knew the hotel allowed others to stay here in his absence.

"The hotel likes me to be happy here." Quinton slanted a glance at the butler, whose function it was never to be out of earshot as long as either Quinton or any of his guests remained in the rooms. "Isn't that right, Jeffers?"

The white-haired man bowed stiffly from the waist, as he had been taught to do at the same school in charge of training the Royal Family's butlers.

"Yes, sir. Zanadu enjoys having its special guests return."

He wasn't one to be taken in easily. Quinton knew the bottom line. And he also knew how to make the most of it. Despite the fact that he could have easily bought and sold everyone in the immediate vicinity, he enjoyed being wooed and given things in an attempt to win his favor. And his bankroll.

"And it's all free," Quinton confided to them with obvious pride.

There was a gleam in his eyes that Whitney was unable to fathom. All she knew was that it was incredibly cold. Ruthless. And self-satisfied. Richard Quinton was a man who couldn't have anything put over on him, she judged. The thought worried her not for her own sake but for Zane's, although she wasn't quite sure why.

"Well," Quinton amended, "free as long as I keep gambling at their tables and leave more than I take." He thought of the past three nights, and the luck these two had brought him. "I have a feeling, though, that this time around, there might be a bill waiting for me at the front desk when I check out." He laughed again, pleased. "Thanks to you two."

It was absurd for a grown man to actually think that his luck depended on the presence of two people standing on his left while he played.

"I don't—" Whitney's protest died abruptly as Quinton took her hand again and squeezed it. Mentally, she counted off a beat, then drew back her hand.

"Don't be modest—you two are my good-luck charms. Both of you." He paused as she slipped her hand from his. For a moment, his eyes darkened before he continued. "Luck is a very real, tangible thing. You either have it within your grasp—" he closed his fingers into a tight fist "—or you don't. I'm convinced that your presence has made Lady Luck linger at my side."

Quinton read her expression correctly. Russell's wife was chafing. It intrigued him. Other women would have played up to him for what they could get. He wasn't ungenerous. That she seemed to want nothing only urged him on.

"It won't be much longer, Mrs. Russell, I assure you. I'll be leaving tomorrow and then you two can continue with your honeymoon." He smiled, a spider admiring the web he'd spun. "Richer than when you first arrived."

He looked pointedly at Zane. Whitney drew the only conclusion that she could. "Then you've decided to let Zane manage your property?"

Though it meant that Zane had attained his goal, the veiled smile slipping across Quinton's mouth made her feel uneasy.

"Indeed I have. He may manage the property." He offered his hand to Zane, sealing the bargain. Quinton had his own set of values, and a man's worth was only as good as his word. But once that was lost, it could never be redeemed. "Good-luck charms have to be polished from time to time." He glanced toward Sally. "Isn't that right, my dear?"

Sally toyed with her earring. One perfect pearl gently swung to and fro against her fingertip. "Whatever you say, Richard."

"That's right," he agreed. "Whatever I say." Business put on hold, Quinton looked from Whitney to Zane and rubbed his hands together. "Well, what will you have? Just name it." He gestured expansively toward the bar. It was actually a delicately carved eighteenth-century piece, imported from Japan. "I assure you that the hotel has stocked it for me. Or, if not, Jeffers here will be more than happy to find it, buy it or steal it for you. You've but to tell him what it is. Isn't that so, Jeffers?"

"Yes, sir."

It was clear that Quinton was flexing his muscles for them. "I'll have a Black Russian," Zane said. He wanted a clear head, but if he asked for anything departing from his normal choice, he knew Quinton would either become suspicious, see it as a bad omen or take offense.

Jeffers promptly located the bottles of Kahlua and vodka and began mixing the drink.

"Water," Whitney requested in quiet rebellion against all the opulence surrounding them. "I'd like some water, please."

Quinton's laugh was deep and throaty. "Then water you shall have, Mrs. Russell. You'll excuse us," he casually tossed at Zane in his wake.

Hand on her shoulder, Quinton ushered Whitney into a private kitchen where two chefs were busy preparing the afternoon meal. Both men glanced toward him as he entered the room with Whitney and murmured subservient hellos before returning to their work.

Standing before the refrigerator, Quinton nodded toward the door. "Open it, please," he instructed. The chef closest to him dropped the knife he was dicing with on the chopping block and hurried to comply.

He really took pleasure in pulling strings and jerking

people around. Suppressing her irritation, Whitney reached to open the door herself.

The hand Quinton placed on her arm was a silent warning. "Don't." Politely issued, it was still a command. "It's what he's paid to do. Let him do it."

Inclining her head, struggling not to say something about pompous asses, Whitney moved aside and let the chef open the refrigerator for them.

Inside, along one long rack, was an assortment of bottled mineral water. Quinton gestured toward them. "Take your pick."

The bottles came in different, muted hues, like a rainbow. Whitney made her selection by crossing to the sink and turning on the tap.

"I like things simple," Whitney told him. "Tap water."

It was a minor challenge, but it was still a challenge. Quinton reached around her and shut off the tap with one quick jerk.

"There's simple, and then there's common. I deal with the common only when I absolutely must." He looked over his shoulder at the anxious chef.

It occurred to Whitney that the man must have witnessed Quinton's darker side at one time or other. It was obvious that he was fearful of another eruption. She held her peace.

Quinton chose a bottle for her. "The lady will sample that one."

With movements exhibiting both desire to please and to avoid any displays of disapproval, the chef quickly removed the pale green bottle from the shelf and opened it. He poured the mineral water into a glass and presented it to Whitney as if it were the finest champagne.

Given everything, it probably cost somewhere in the

same neighborhood. She took a sip and thought that she actually liked tap water better.

"Good?"

She knew Quinton was in no mood for a debate. That made two of them. "Yes."

"See?" He took her by the elbow and ushered from the room. It was a signal for the work in the kitchen to begin again.

"Would you like to join the others?" Quinton asked, "Or shall I take you on a personal tour of my accommodations?"

She had no doubt where the tour would end. Whitney didn't relish the thought of having to wrestle with Quinton. She looked toward the living room.

"Why don't we do both?" she proposed. "In that order?"

She'd managed, for the moment, to block his move. He enjoyed a good game of chess as much as the next man. "Very well."

Sally was hitting on him. Subtly, tastefully, but a man knew when he was being hit on, and Sally was most definitely making her intentions known. Under the guise of showing him different artifacts that were displayed on the shelves that ran along the length of one wall, she'd reached for an item and brushed against Zane twice. Brushed her body against his. Waiting for the unspoken invitation to garner some sort of response from him.

Not in a million years, lady. I like my body parts just where they are, he thought.

And Zane had no doubt that if he were, insanely, of a mind to see just how willing a lady Sally really was when it came to playing doctor, Quinton would gut him like a freshly caught salmon.

He was relieved when he saw Whitney and Quinton reenter the room.

Zane crossed to Whitney and slipped his arm around her shoulders. "I was beginning to think that maybe you got lost."

Quinton gestured about the area with the nonchalance of someone who had grown accustomed to wealth and couldn't imagine anything else. "It's not really that big. It's all relative, actually. This place could occupy a corner of my home in Bel Air."

Whitney didn't doubt it. "You provide guests with compasses at the door?"

Quinton laughed, amused. "You know, Russell, your wife is far more delightful than I originally surmised." His eyes were warm, yet calculating, as they regarded Whitney. "You seem different than you did when I first met you."

That would be the amnesia, she thought. She wondered what she'd said to him to generate his initial reaction. "It takes me a while to get comfortable."

Nice save, Zane thought.

Quinton sipped his dry martini, watching her over the rim of his glass. "And are you? Comfortable?"

She smiled at him. *Like someone running barefoot over a field of cacti.*

"How could I not be, when my hosts are so charming?" She and Sally exchanged looks. In a way, she had a feeling that the other woman understood her. They both knew that the way around Quinton was to keep his ego anointed.

Jeffers appeared in the doorway, bowing formally as he announced, "Brunch is served, sir."

Quinton presented his arm to Whitney. "Shall we?"

Zane offered his to Sally, who took it gladly.

* * *

The meal, like the suite, had to be seen to be believed. The chefs retained by the hotel to oversee Quinton's kitchen during his stay at Zanadu prepared fare that no ordinary restaurant could readily include on its menu. Not without charging the exorbitant prices that few could afford to pay.

And Quinton was getting it all free, Whitney thought, compliments of a grateful management. There were little gifts from exclusive shops throughout the rooms. And private limousines, not to mention a jet, at his disposal, night or day. Somehow, it just didn't seem right. He certainly had enough money to pay for all this. It probably would have represented no more than spare change to him.

"It's just good business on their part," Quinton told her when she commented on the lobster that had been flown in fresh from Maine just this morning when he'd expressed a desire for it. "I'm what they call a high roller." He looked at the expressionless butler who was serving them. "Isn't that right, Jeffers?"

The butler never missed a beat as he presented the dish of lobster Newburg to Zane. "That is rather an indelicate term, Mr. Quinton. The hotel prefers to think of you as an honored patron."

And Quinton knew just how the honor had been earned. "Who's been known to drop a cool million in less than an hour."

She knew that Quinton gambled huge sums of money the way the people in the lobby played the dollar machines, but she'd never thought that much money was involved. He was talking about sums that any random twenty people collectively didn't see in a lifetime.

"How would you do that?" She'd almost said "could" instead.

He passed her remark off as an annoying inconvenience. But Whitney had seen the look on his face each time the house had been the winner. Quinton wasn't a man who liked to lose.

"By having Lady Luck turn her back on me just as the cards were being dealt." He held his glass up, waiting for Jeffers to refill it for him. With flawless movements, Jeffers ceased serving lobster and picked up the bottle of wine. Quinton raised the filled glass and toasted first Whitney, then Zane. "I knew the minute that you pushed me out of the way of that car that there was something special about you."

You couldn't have known it at the time, Zane thought. "When I shoved you aside, you had a few choice words for me," Zane reminded him.

Quinton shrugged, sampling the freshened glass. "Oh, that. I'm not accustomed to being handled." He looked pointedly at Sally, then shifted his gaze to Whitney. "Unless I specifically request it, that is."

The man certainly was blunt, Whitney thought. And accustomed to getting what he wanted. She wondered how long he would take no for an answer before he tired of being polite about it.

"I didn't have time to shout a warning," Zane said. "If I hadn't pushed you out of the way, you would have been flattened. I thought your bodyguard was going to shoot me." He laughed now, but it had been a chilling moment. The man had whipped out his pistol from a shoulder holster and had trained it on Zane a second before the car had come rolling down.

Quinton nodded. "If the car hadn't gotten in the way, he would have. He's no longer with me," he added matter-of-factly. "There didn't seem to be much point in keeping a man around who couldn't do his job."

Whitney wondered if the man had been drawn and quartered or merely fired.

"I'm thinking of offering one of those two gentlemen out front the job when I leave. It has to be better than standing around in multicolored harem pants." Quinton pushed himself away from the table. He looked at his guests, ignoring Sally. "Well, can I offer anyone anything else?"

Whitney had done the food justice. Not caring for her host had no effect on her appetite. But even she had a limit. "Not unless you want to see me explode."

Quinton had watched her sample everything. "I like to see a woman with a hearty appetite. It speaks well of her." He nodded toward his mistress. "Sally eats like a bird. I don't care for a picky eater."

"You also don't care for a fat woman," Sally reminded him casually.

Sally knew what was necessary to remain on Quinton's good side. She'd tasted the kind of life he had to offer and had vowed not to be discarded, like her predecessors, no matter what it took. She had the stomach to do what was needed when it was needed. She knew that was her chief asset as far as Quinton was concerned. That and the blind eye she turned to his continual dalliances.

"It's true, I don't," Quinton agreed. "I have a weakness for shapely, pretty things." He let his eyes linger on Whitney. "Now then, shall we see about that tour?"

Five minutes into the tour, Whitney began to see why there was a staff on hand. It was to keep Quinton and his mistress from getting lost on the premises. She felt as if she should leave breadcrumbs in her wake to retrace her steps.

It wasn't a suite, in her estimation. Suites could easily be explored in a few minutes. Quinton's accommodations were more like a house. A subpalace, as the management preferred to call it. A palace fit for a king, for a king's ransom.

Or, in this case, a king's ransom lost. It didn't make sense to her, spending this sort of money to keep someone like Quinton happy; but then, she didn't have the vantage point of someone running a gambling establishment. All she saw was one greedy, selfish man.

Listening to Quinton talk about himself and his tastes for the past two hours had given her an incredible headache, even though he spoke in measured, cultured tones.

She'd grown quiet, Zane realized. He wondered if she was feeling well.

He wasn't the only one who had noticed. "You look pained, my dear. Surely it's not because of something you ate."

She moved her head slightly, with little feeling. Any sudden movement would have had the tiny hammers turning into the sledge variety. "Oh, no, everything was wonderful. I just have a headache."

"There is an entire pharmacy at our disposal. Whatever you need, I can supply."

She was sure he could, or at least that he thought he could. Everything in the matching his and hers bathrooms was oversized—and no doubt overstocked. But what she wanted was to leave this tastefully decorated mausoleum and lie down.

"I'm afraid that nothing ever does any good. The only remedy that works for me is to get some rest and sleep it off."

Quinton indicated the winding staircase. "You have your choice of several beds."

She would be as tense as a surfboard, anticipating his appearance at any moment if she took him up on his offer. She wanted to avoid that at all costs.

"Thank you, but I'd really rather just lie down in my own room, if you don't mind." Zane began to rise. She placed a hand on his shoulder, pushing him down again. "No, honey, you stay. This might be a good time for you and Mr. Quinton to review your agreement." She subtly made reference to the promise Quinton had tendered to Zane earlier. "There's no reason you have to hang around the room, watching me sleep."

Besides, if Zane were there, she knew she wouldn't get any rest. She might have the beginnings of a major headache, but she wasn't dead.

A slight line of impatience creased Quinton's brow. "Are you certain I can't offer you something?"

She paused, thinking. "Well, there is one thing."

"And that would be—?"

"A guide. I think I need help finding the door." She wasn't sure if she was supposed to turn left or right after leaving the dining room. The tour had only served to confuse her waning sense of direction.

Waving Jeffers away, Quinton presented her with his arm. "I'll take you there myself."

Zane didn't like the thought of Whitney going off by herself. But this would give him an opportunity to get Quinton alone to talk business. Without Whitney around, Quinton would probably retreat with him to the den, leaving Sally to amuse herself.

Which she probably could do quite well, Zane mused, given the opportunity.

"Are you sure you'll be all right?" Zane asked Whitney.

He was sweet to worry. "I'll be fine. All I need is some rest."

"I'll look in on you in a little while," Zane promised as she left the room.

"Take your time," she told him.

"That's what I like, an understanding woman." Quinton nodded his approval as he escorted her to the door. "I could have a physician look in on you," he offered.

That was the last thing she wanted, to be fussed over. "It's a headache, Mr. Quinton, not a hernia. I'll be fine with a little sleep."

He toyed with the locket she wore, being far too familiar for her liking. "Then you'll be able to come to the casino tonight?"

It was hard to reconcile superstitions with a man who considered himself so dynamic in every other way. "I wouldn't miss it," she promised, wishing that she could.

Quinton signaled for the butler. "Jeffers will take you to your room."

"There's no need for that." Not waiting for him, she opened the front door herself. "I'm sure he has more important things to tend to. And I've been walking around on my own for quite a few years now." She paused. "Thank you for brunch—it was wonderful. I'll see you later." She smiled just as she slipped out. "Send back my husband when you're through with him."

"When I'm satisfied with his answers," Quinton said to the closed door.

On the other side of the door, Whitney heard him and wondered what he meant by that.

Maybe, Whitney thought twenty minutes later, she shouldn't have turned down Quinton's offer of an aspirin. The headache had refused to abate and she was getting desperate. Quinton probably had fifty different brands to choose from. And there certainly didn't seem to be any anywhere in the suite. She'd gone through the medicine cabinet and her own luggage twice, checking along the cloth perimeter. But apart from an extra toothbrush stuck in the lining, it was empty.

Sighing, she set both suitcases back in the closet beside Zane's. She eyed the tan luggage, thinking. Maybe Zane had packed a bottle. She took it out and placed his suitcase on the bed, then went through it systematically.

The thorough search yielded the same result. Nothing. With a sigh, she dropped down onto the bed. The suitcase slid off, landing on the floor with a thud as one edge caught the corner of the bed. She debated just letting it lie there, then reached for it. The headache pounded harder.

And that was when she saw it.

There was a gun on the floor. It had just fallen out of the empty suitcase.

Chapter 11

For a moment, all Whitney could do was stare at it. Her brain refused to accept what her eyes saw.

But it was there, at her feet. A gun. And it had fallen out of Zane's suitcase. From a hidden compartment that somehow must have opened when it had hit the foot of the bed. Why else hadn't she found it when she'd searched the interior for aspirin?

Hidden. Zane had a gun he kept hidden.

Why? What did he need with a gun?

The muscles in her stomach tightened like a clenched fist, bunching so hard that it was difficult for her to breathe. Just what kind of a man had she fallen in love with and married?

Like a desperate, cornered man, her mind began to grasp at half theories in an attempt to find a way to exonerate him.

But all she managed to do was condemn him.

Dragging a deep breath into her lungs, she followed

it with another and another, until her breathing had steadied again.

But her hands were still shaking as she picked up the gun. The feel of the cool steel against her fingers brought with it a flash of a memory that raced through her brain with lightning speed.

She'd done this before—held a gun in her hand just like this. But when? And why?

Whitney couldn't begin to think of a single reason why she should be familiar with handguns. Or with any sort of weapon, for that matter.

Or why Zane should have one in his possession.

The memory, like the glimmer of the early-morning sun between the leaves of spring trees, disappeared. She couldn't summon it back no matter how hard she concentrated. Holding the gun didn't help. It only magnified her feeling of despair.

She had nowhere to go, no one to turn to. She had only herself and she didn't even know who that was. Whitney struggled to pull herself together. She couldn't afford to go to pieces now.

Pieces. She was holding pieces, only a few pieces in her hand and the puzzle before her comprised more than five thousand. She had no idea how any of it fitted together.

All she knew was that there had to be more.

There had to be something that she had overlooked. Something that she was obviously missing.

Besides her mind.

Quinton leaned back in the roomy, wine-colored chair that complimented the ornately carved eighteenth-century desk. Leaned and rocked as its soft-as-butter leather molded about him like the embrace of a well-cared-for mistress. He'd already made up his mind about Zane and the proposition, but he always left an escape route for himself. Just in case. When things looked too good, too pat, they usually were.

But not always. Sometimes the perfect hand did get dealt. Quinton just had to decide whether this was that time.

Straightening, he opened the humidor on the desk and tilted the container toward Zane. Cigars stood at attention within it like a well-drilled brigade of soldiers.

"Have one." He waited for Zane to make his selection.

Pretending to actually debate over his choice, Zane picked one. Offering a cigar from his private collection was Quinton's way of sealing a bargain. To pass it up would have been an insult, flying in the face of one of his many superstitions. Zane had worked too hard and come too far to do that, even though the idea of inserting one of these fat aromatic cylinders into his mouth and lighting it repulsed him.

He had never had a smoking habit he needed to break. There were other things to haunt him, to shackle him, but this minor vice had never been one of them. He didn't smoke at all, not even occasionally.

Zane hoped he wouldn't embarrass himself.

Quinton passed his small scissors to Zane after using them to cut off the tip of his cigar. Zane mimicked the action deftly. With an approving nod, Quinton leaned over to light Zane's cigar, then brought the flame back to his own. He slipped the engraved gold lighter into his pocket and took a long, thoughtful puff.

There was no one else in the room to light the cigars, or to jump in anticipation of Quinton's next need. Here they were alone in a room meant for conversation and reflection.

A room where deals were struck. A room that Quinton had regularly checked for hidden transmission devices.

Quinton leaned back and pursed his lips, blowing. Smoke swirled in the air above his head like an ironic halo. His eyes narrowed into pensive slits as he studied Zane over the tip of his cigar. You could tell a lot about a man by the way he smoked another man's cigar. Just as you could by the way he did or didn't refuse the attentions of another man's woman.

He thought of Sally and smiled to himself. Russell had passed that test.

Quinton nodded at the humidor. "They bring these in for me daily. Sweating all the way." He laughed as he thought of the furtive way Jeffers looked around as he produced the Havana cigars each afternoon. "The butler's as straight as an arrow. Hates the idea of being party to anything illegal."

Quinton paused, reflecting. The butler, like the rest of the world, was there for his personal use. Quinton gave the man less than no thought ordinarily, now that he was satisfied that Jeffers checked out.

"Probably doesn't even cheat on his taxes." Quinton laughed softly to himself. Zane thought it was a particularly nasty sound. "Where would we be if everyone was like that?"

The answer was automatic. "Out of business."

Meticulously, Quinton flicked ashes into an ashtray shaped like a leering gargoyle, taking care that none fell on the desk. He didn't like seeing fine things marred— unless it was unavoidable.

"Thank God the average citizen finds it easier to be corrupted than to live the life of a saint." He watched

Zane's expression. "I'd find that boring, wouldn't you? Being a saint."

He was probing him, Zane thought. Trying to make him lower his guard and then get inside his head. "Fortunately, I've never had that problem."

This time the laugh was genuine. "Good answer. Neither have I." A gleam entered Quinton's gray eyes. "I like living on the edge."

Zane looked around at the wall of books Quinton had insisted on, some of them first editions. And at the vase, which held flowers that were brought in daily. A history buff, Zane recognized the design. The vase was worth thousands of dollars. These were the surroundings of a man who enjoyed the finer, softer things of life.

"I wouldn't exactly call this the edge." The edge was a Spartan place, a place where the faint of heart never tread, falling back instead on the familiar, the comforting. The edge didn't have bottles of wine whose cost rivaled the national debt.

"But it is," Quinton contradicted. He gestured around the room with his cigar. "This is what the edge can get you—if you've got the stomach to play the game." He pulled the smoke into his mouth and savored it before releasing it again. "You hold the cards close to your chest. Is the other guy bluffing?" He smiled craftily. "Are you? Gets the adrenaline pumping. The only game in town worth playing, Russell." He rocked, thinking, remembering. Reliving. "The only game."

Zane thought of Sally. A man didn't shower a woman with expensive gifts if she didn't mean something to him on some level. He doubted that Quinton knew what love was, but he'd be willing to bet that lust and the satisfaction of it were high on his list.

"I thought sex might figure into that somewhere."

Carefully, he drew the smoke into his mouth and then slowly blew it out. Zane congratulated himself for not choking.

Quinton thought of Russell's wife. The woman had a tight little rear he wouldn't mind fondling. He wondered if Russell was subtly offering her to him the way he'd offered Russell his cigars.

"Sex is part of it," he agreed. "A nice little dividend. You play the game right and all the trappings come to you. But I suppose I don't have to tell you that, do I?"

Zane was going to be glad when this was over. He felt like a fly that had nearly managed, against all odds, to traverse the spider's web and make it to the other side without getting captured or devoured. That was his goal. To make it to the other side without getting caught or eliminated.

"No, you don't," Zane agreed.

It was time to draw the discussion to a close, Quinton decided. He was, after all, on his vacation, and this was business. He rose. "I'll have the goods ready for you just before I leave."

There was something in Quinton's voice that tipped him off. "You have them here?"

Quinton deliberately ignored the question. He hadn't gotten to where he was by letting anyone else have too much information. It was his to dole out as the need required. There was no need here.

"I'll have them ready for you before I leave," Quinton repeated. "Unless I change my mind." Possession put him in the driver's seat.

He'd overstepped his bounds, Zane realized, and he was having his hand slapped. The point was not to ask too many questions and arouse Quinton's annoyance.

"Hope that doesn't happen." Zane voiced the sentiment with enough contrition mixed with confidence to carry it off. Quinton seemed mildly impressed at how coolly he handled himself.

"And of course you'll have the money when the exchange is made?"

Zane didn't blink an eye, even though the smoke stung. "Of course."

Quinton didn't like being in the dark. The dark was something that he was supposed to utilize, not inhabit. "It's not in your suite."

Nothing appeared to have been disturbed within the suite, but Zane had no doubts that Quinton had already had the room searched. That was why the money was being held elsewhere for safekeeping. Sheridan had made the drop for him. A valise filled with the amount they had agreed on, an amount Zane had subtly engineered Quinton to accept, was in the safe of another hotel.

The smile on Zane's mouth matched Quinton's. Cool, unshakable. "No, it's not."

Quinton's smile deepened, a hint of underlying steel evident. "You remind me a little of me when I was first starting out."

He was a man who was difficult to read. Zane wasn't sure whether Quinton was offering friendship or being cutting. "I'm not a novice, Mr. Quinton, if that's what you mean. But I'll take that as a compliment."

"You should." Quinton was growing tired of the conversation. "All right, then it's settled. We'll make the exchange just before I leave. I'm partial to noon." That taken care of, Quinton dismissed him. "You can go, Russell." Rising, he walked in front of Zane to the door. "I expect to see you with your wife at the casino this evening."

Pausing, his hand on the knob, Quinton looked at Zane. "She doesn't know anything about this, does she?" It was an assumption, not a question. There was nothing in the woman's manner to indicate that she suspected.

Zane shook his head. "Only what I tell her."

It was what Quinton wanted to hear. "Keep it that way. Women just tend to get things tangled up. I find they serve their purpose best when kept on a short leash."

Zane wondered what Whitney would have said about that philosophy. Given her nature, or her nature before she'd fallen on the balcony, she would have felt compelled to show Quinton just how much damage she could do, even tethered on a short leash.

He'd give anything to be able to see that, Zane mused. Taking the hand Quinton offered, he shook it. "I'll try to remember that."

Zane hurried up to his suite. He'd felt uneasy all during the negotiations with Quinton. It hadn't had anything to do with Quinton himself, which, Zane knew, was a mistake in itself. He should have kept his mind entirely on the deal being negotiated and remained on his guard. That was why he was here in the first place.

But even as terms were being reviewed, Zane found his mind drifting to Whitney. She was the source of his unease.

He didn't like leaving her alone for any length of time. Zane wanted to be around her, to filter any information that might come her way and act as a buffer. Though it sounded suspiciously like Quinton's philosophy, it had nothing to do with keeping her on a leash. It was just that he was so close to pulling this off, Zane didn't want to take a chance on Whitney somehow killing the deal.

Killing.

It was an appropriate word in this case. Zane didn't delude himself that Quinton had taken a parental liking to him. Quinton was the type of man who could coolly have eliminated anyone who displeased him for any reason, real or imagined. His reputation struck fear into men's hearts, and with good cause. Richard Quinton had power at his disposal. Power that could very easily ruin lives, as well as end them.

Quinton was definitely not a man you wanted to get on the wrong side of. Not unless you had a .38 in your hands.

The elevator doors opened on his floor and Zane hurried out. He couldn't shake the feeling that something was wrong.

He could feel it as he walked down the hall. The back of his neck itched again. He ran his hand over it and looked around, expecting to find that he was being watched.

But there was no one in the hall. No convenient maid pushing a cleaning cart, no bellman seeming to hurry toward another destination. No evidence of a surveillance camera.

That didn't mean that there wasn't one somewhere on the floor, although he'd had Sheridan check the layout thoroughly before he'd booked this suite. The surveillance cameras didn't necessarily have to belong to the hotel. Quinton was a sophisticated man with highly trained, intelligent people in his employ.

Which was why Zane was careful of every word he uttered.

He hoped to hell that Quinton hadn't entertained himself by watching him with Whitney. The thought hadn't occurred to him until just now. Now that it did, Zane could feel his anger rising. He reined it in. No sense in getting himself worked up on a supposition. He had enough to worry about.

Zane unlocked the door quietly, wondering if he'd find Whitney asleep. If she was, he didn't want to wake her until it was almost time to leave for the casino.

She wasn't asleep. She was awake.

And he had an entirely different problem to deal with.

Whitney was sitting on the bed, rigid. Exactly as she had been for the past half hour. She was obviously waiting for him to return.

On her lap was his backup weapon.

Zane silently cursed himself. Somehow he must have gotten careless.

Zane slipped the suite card into his pocket. "What do you have there?" he asked lightly, as if he were inquiring about a new pair of shoes she'd just purchased.

When he bent to kiss her cheek, Whitney pulled her head back. Her surprise and disbelief had had time to simmer and settle. Her anger was now stone cold and all the more formidable for it.

"You know what this is. No games, Zane." She took the gun in both hands and held it up to him. "This was in your suitcase. What was it doing in there?"

Unable to answer immediately, he countered with an offensive of his own. "What were you doing in my suitcase?"

But she was on to him. "No diversions, Zane, no tantalizing sex romps to get me off course. You're not allowed to ask any questions, only answer them. I want the truth. What are you doing with a gun?" She enunciated each word of the question slowly, letting them sink in one by one.

Zane shoved his hands into his pockets, digging deeper than the fabric. Thinking fast. "I need it to protect myself."

She wasn't buying it. At least, not without details. "What does a land developer have to protect himself from? Rabid squirrels?"

He didn't rise to the bait. His voice was as calm as hers was heated. "I didn't tell you about this because I didn't want to upset you."

That was certainly ironic. "Well, you failed. I'm upset. I'm very upset." She looked down at the weapon, then at him. Was he out of his mind? What was he thinking? "What are you doing with this? Carrying around guns is illegal."

He shook his head. "I've got a permit." Just not on him. What he was carrying on him was another gun, a smaller one that was easily accessible.

That didn't make any sense. "If you have a permit, why was the gun hidden?"

"I told you, I didn't want to upset you. Besides, this isn't Dodge City, Whit. You don't exactly wear a gun strapped on your hip anymore."

His voice was low, soothing, with just a hint of an apology in it. It amazed him how well he could carry it off. But he still hated lying to her like this. He'd never had to before. Except about one thing and that hadn't been a verbal lie. Only one that he had lived. He realized that now more than ever.

He reached for the weapon but didn't take it. He had no way of knowing if she had loaded it. "May I?"

She raised her hands away from it. "Take it. Throw it away."

He picked it up by its barrel and carefully replaced it in his suitcase. The false bottom had somehow come undone. He thought of Quinton and what he'd said about the money not being in the suite.

Looked as if his men hadn't found the gun. If they had, he knew they would have taken it.

"They don't like you just throwing guns away." He slid the closet door closed again. "I think it comes under the same heading as disposing of paint and inflammable cleaning fluids."

She felt cold. Cold and bereft. How could she trust him when there were things he wouldn't tell her? What else was there that she didn't know?

"This isn't funny, Zane."

He sat down beside her on the bed. Her body stiffened. Zane tried to curb his anger.

"No, it's not funny," he agreed. He took her hand in his. When she pulled it away, he took it again. And this time held it firmly. "But you have to understand, I was afraid for my life. And yours."

"Mine?" She stared at him, completely confused. "Why?" And then it came to her. "Does this have anything to do with Quinton?"

He wanted to tell her. Wanted to tell her so badly that the words formed and hovered on his tongue. He was close, so close.

And then he looked into her eyes and lied. "No, it doesn't. It has to do with Madeline." The fact that he could it so smoothly told him he was good at what he did.

Right now, he wasn't exactly crazy about his job.

But she couldn't know the truth yet. Not until he had the cocaine in his possession and Quinton had the money in his.

Madeline was his mother's name. A name he would always remember, even if her face had long disappeared into the murky recesses of time, erasing all trace from his memory. He couldn't remember what she looked like, no matter how hard he tried. But then, he'd only been about four when she'd walked out on him.

It still wasn't making any sense to Whitney. "Madeline? Who's Madeline?"

"My former girlfriend. The woman you made me forget."

Very tenderly, Zane touched her cheek. What had started out as an explosion of chemistry had come down to this. Love. He was in love with her. Gut-wrenchingly in love.

And it wasn't going to matter to her, once she knew. She probably wouldn't even believe him. It was the price he paid for keeping her safe.

Getting his mind back on the story he was fabricating, Zane continued. "The woman who swore she wouldn't be forgotten. She stalked me, Whitney. And threatened to kill both of us if she ever found us together. I got a restraining order against her, but Madeline's not the kind who'd let a legal document get in the way of what she wants."

Why hadn't he said anything about this before? Or had he? No, he couldn't have. He was acting as if this was the first time he was telling her about this. Her anger melted. She began to think how awful this must have been for him, holding back a secret because he wanted to protect her. She didn't want to be protected; she wanted to help him.

"You're being stalked?"

"I was. Madeline hasn't been around in the past month, but I'm still not convinced she won't turn up.

She doesn't usually give up easily. Knowing I had a gun around made me feel a little better. It gives me an edge on her.''

She looked toward the closet. ''Doesn't do much good in the suitcase.''

''It's a precaution.'' He looked at Whitney and told her the truth. ''I don't want to take a chance on anything happening to you.''

He made her feel loved and cherished. ''Nothing's going to happen to me,'' she said with such confidence that for a moment he thought her memory had returned. ''And we'll face this thing together. I don't know what I was like before. Probably a hothouse flower, from all the indications I'm picking up from you.''

Zane tried not to smile. The complete opposite was true.

''But all that's going to change. I don't want to be just your wife, Zane. I want to be your partner. In everything.'' She turned her face up to his. ''No more secrets.''

Oh, God, Whitney, why are you making this so hard?

''No more secrets,'' he promised and wished he could bite off his tongue. All the reasons he had for the lie didn't seem to want to hold up. Not in the face of the look in her eyes.

That resolved, curiosity nibbled at her. ''What was she like?''

He shrugged, buying himself a little time. The fewer details he gave her, the less he'd have to remember. The list was already too long.

''Just someone passing through my life. No one important. Not like you.'' He pressed a kiss to her temple. ''How's your headache?''

It had disappeared. She hadn't even noticed it go. Her mouth curved. "I think you cured it."

Maybe he could buy himself a little more time. A little more of heaven before he was cast down into hell for all eternity. He slipped his arms around her. "Anything else aching that I can cure?"

The smile began in her eyes. "Well, now that you mention it—"

Chapter 12

Deep-seated satisfaction mingled with exhaustion, suffusing her. This had to be what a marathon runner reaching the finish line felt like.

Whitney could hardly move.

A smile drifted over her face as she looked at the man beside her on the floor. They'd blazed a trail through the suite and had wound up just at the foot of the bed, never quite managing to get into it. It didn't matter. Anywhere she was was paradise, as long as Zane was with her.

With a sigh of contentment, she feathered her fingers through his hair.

"You know, I feel as if I've known you forever. Like we've been soul mates for a very long time." Whitney smiled at her own words. "I guess that's kind of odd, isn't it?" Summoning a wisp of strength, she propped herself up on her elbow to look at him. "I mean, to feel as if we've been together for a long time when we haven't. You said that we had a whirlwind romance. I just met you New Year's Eve and this is... What month is it, anyway?" She realized that she hadn't a clue.

Zane watched her expression as she spoke. She was so animated that he could see her feelings chasing one another across her face. It made him feel tired just to look at her.

No, he amended, that wasn't the only reason he felt as if he'd been ridden hard and put away wet. Whitney had a little something to do with that. And with the way he felt in other respects. Guilt was never far out of the picture.

"Beginning of June."

"June," she repeated, as if saying the month out loud would help the information sink into her head. "Not even six months." The smile curving her lips filtered through her body. Or was that the other way around? she mused. All she knew was that she felt hopelessly in love and very grateful for this exquisite feeling humming in her veins. "Not exactly a lifetime."

He didn't want to talk about the lies he'd fed her. Hearing them repeated only racked rusty nails over his conscience.

"It's all relative." Zane leaned over her. The weight of his upper body pressed against her, pinning her to the floor. "For a butterfly, that's half a lifetime. For a fruit fly, we're talking hundreds of generations. Maybe thousands." He let his fingers slide along her cheek. God, he loved her. And he was going to pay for it. "I was never all that good in math."

She hooted at the admission, amused. "And you work with money?"

He passed it off lightly, lifting a careless shoulder in acknowledgment. "I know how many zeros there are in a million."

Whitney's eyes widened. She hadn't really given the deal Zane was trying to solidify with Quinton that much thought in terms of dollars and cents, only in terms of inconvenience. Hearing what was involved sobered her for a moment.

"Is that how much this deal is all about? A million dollars?"

Actually, it was about three times that, but he had a feeling that saying so might have aroused her suspicions. He didn't want any more questions that might trip him up. No more questions until it was over.

He looked at a spot just above her head and nodded. "My commission on the houses sold if the development goes through."

She whistled softly. "No wonder you were eager to get Quinton to like you."

But Quinton and his money were miles away from their room as far as she was concerned. At least for now. She sighed as she shifted and felt Zane's body move with hers. The crackle of electricity began all over again, slowly, seductively.

Her eyes caressed his face. "Do we have to get dressed yet?"

Zane didn't want to get dressed. He didn't want to move. All he wanted was to remain beside her like this, forever.

"No, we have about ninety minutes before we have to meet Quinton at the casino." Tonight there would be a private game in one of the rooms set aside for only a few players. Quinton hadn't used exact words, but their presence was mandatory.

Whitney noticed that Zane didn't mention Sally and wondered if that was an oversight, or if the woman wasn't coming. Either way, that was something to think about later. Right now, there were more important things on her mind.

"Ninety minutes." Her eyes on his, she slowly ran her tongue over her lips. She saw the response she wanted. "Do you know that I can get dressed in five minutes?"

He laughed softly, then kissed her shoulder. There was no way he was ever going to get enough of her. "Ten, I've timed you."

She could be flexible. Whitney inclined her head. "All right, for the sake of argument, let's say ten minutes." Her body moved toward his invitingly. "What do you figure we should do with the other eighty minutes we have left?"

Whitney took his breath away. Who would have ever thought that beneath that cool, competent exterior was this insatiable goddess?

"Get our strength back?" he proposed tentatively.

"You mean I've weakened you already?" Whitney shook her head in sorrowful disbelief. "Zane, where's your stamina?"

Zane spared a glance over his shoulder. The room looked as if a hurricane had hit it. Once they had begun making love, it was as if flames had ignited. They'd made love on top of any flat surface they found in the suite. Over and over again. They made love on the desk, in the shower, on the floor.

Each time they reached an end, one of them would provoke the other and the delicious journey began all over again. But this time, Zane had been certain they were both completely depleted.

Zane looked at her again. "I left my stamina somewhere in the rubble, I think."

She wove her arms around his neck, moving entic-

ingly beneath him. She didn't have to have full possession of her memory to know she'd never felt like this
before about a man.

"You're not going to start disappointing me now, are
you, Zane?"

She was teasing, but her question drove a shaft
through his conscience. Or was that his heart? "No," he
told Whitney quietly, "not yet."

She shivered suddenly as a chill passed over her heart.
"You looked so serious when you said that." He was
smiling at her, but there was something beneath that. She
could have sworn it. "Zane, is there something that
you're keeping from me?"

Damn, he was an idiot. Why had he said that to her?
Zane shook his head. "No, I think I've given you absolutely all that I've got to give. For all intents and purposes, I think I'm dead."

Maybe she'd just imagined that he was keeping something from her. And she didn't want to let it ruin what
time they had left before they had to make their mandatory appearance at the casino.

Whitney slanted her eyes down along his anatomy.
They shone as she raised them again to his face. "Mind
if I have a stab at it?"

He laughed. "Only if that's not what you actually
intend to do."

She'd probably always loved a challenge, Whitney decided. This one invigorated her.

"No, what I intend to do is this."

Ever so lightly, Whitney brushed her lips against his
throat, arching so that her breasts brushed tantalizingly
against his chest. She could feel his reaction to her, in
the shift of his weight, in the warming of his skin. He

wasn't nearly as dead as he professed to be. And he was going to become less dead by the moment.

"And this."

Still moving her body in erotic waves against his, Whitney glided just the tip of her tongue along his lips. As he opened his mouth to kiss her, she suddenly pulled away and then used his surprise to her advantage. With the agility of a cat, she reversed their positions, her body pinning his.

When he tried to get up, she pressed the flat of her hand against his sternum, keeping him in place, a captured trophy.

"And maybe this."

Her breath hot against his belly, Whitney watched the spasm work across it, his muscles tightening in anticipation. Her mouth spread in a self-satisfied smile as she moved first just her lips along Zane's waist, then her tongue, anointing his skin here and there ever so lightly.

The effects were dramatic. He'd ripened, ready for her. Whitney felt her own excitement growing as the game progressed.

Zane reached for her, wanting to drag her back up, wanting to make love to her mouth, her eyes, her face. Wanting to worship her body with his hands and every fiber of his soul.

She felt his hands on her shoulders, his fingers digging in as she moved along his skin, edging lower, ever lower. Her descent was foreshadowed by the light sweep of the edges of her hair along his body.

She was testing him, driving him to the limits. He wasn't sure how much longer he could hold himself in check. Zane groaned. It was an animal sound, half agony, half ecstasy. It sounded very much, she realized, like her name.

Whitney raised her head to look at him.

He ground out each word. "For Pete's sake, Whit, have a little mercy."

"Oh, but I do." Her reply skimmed along his skin, already slick with anticipation. "I have a little mercy. Very little."

Hands cupping him, she gently massaged, then brought her mouth down to him.

Unable to withstand the assault any longer without consequences, Zane grasped Whitney by her shoulders and dragged her back to his level. The feel of her body sliding along his had every nerve ending tensing, bracing. Yearning for release.

He was completely besotted with her. Desire drummed so strongly that he could barely focus on her face.

"You're a witch, you know that? A witch who's spun an incredible spell over me." Zane never thought he could actually love anyone, but he loved her. Completely, hopelessly and irrevocably.

That's what made it so terrible.

He had to tell her, now, while she was so warm and willing in his arms, while there was still a chance that she could understand his reasons. If he told her in the cold light of day, when her heart and her body weren't heated, weren't his, she might never forgive him and that would be more than he could endure.

He'd never thought much about courage. It was just there when he needed it. Except now. Now he felt empty. As shaky as a kid on his first two-wheeler.

"Whit."

Whitney looked into his eyes, her body vibrating from wanting him. Slowly, she saw it. Something in his eyes that made her afraid.

"What?"

The words wouldn't come. They just refused to form on his tongue. He wanted her too much. And was afraid that she would turn away, even now. And he needed her. He didn't think it was physically possible to want a woman so much after having made love with her for the better part of the afternoon, but he did.

Desperately.

And if he told her, she might leave. It shamed him, but he was too much of a coward to risk it. He'd risked his life, faced certain death more than once, but he was afraid to have her turn away from him.

Every man had his limits and she was his.

"What?" she repeated. Whitney pressed a kiss first to one side of his mouth, then to the other, as if to coax the words out. "Tell me."

He couldn't. God help him, he couldn't. Not yet.

Zane filled his hands with her hair, wondering if this was the last time he would touch her like this, like an intimate lover. Quinton was leaving tomorrow. The exchange would be made then. There would be no more reason to go on pretending.

By all rights, he would still have tonight, but he'd learned a long time ago not to count on anything. That way, he wouldn't be disappointed.

But he had learned to count on Whitney, a small voice whispered along the parameters of his mind. Even before now, he'd learn to count on her.

He wasn't as strong as he had thought.

Zane shook his head. "I don't think that eighty minutes is enough."

It wasn't what he was going to say. She knew it, but she let it pass, going instead on the path he'd opened.

Afraid, perhaps, of what he was going to tell her. "I thought you were exhausted."

"I was." But he wasn't any longer. It was as if Whitney was pure adrenaline, injected straight into his veins. "I think you could probably raise the dead if you tried."

She laughed in response, and the room sang with the sound.

It was a wonderful sound, he thought. A sound he would always remember. As he would this afternoon.

"If eighty minutes is all we have," Whitney said philosophically, "then we'll just have to make the most of it, won't we?"

It was his turn to surprise her. Moving as swiftly as a leopard that had sighted his prey, he flipped her over onto her back. "My sentiments on the matter exactly."

Before she could speak, Zane covered her mouth with his. He lost himself in the scent and the taste of her. Wanting desperately not to think, only to experience, to revel in what was so bountifully given him.

And what would, all too soon, be abruptly ripped away again. She wouldn't forgive him. Not for this. He knew her too well.

She'd initiated the foreplay, wanting to arouse him, but now she was the one who was caught in the trap that she had so painstakingly laid out. She was the one being aroused to a frenzy.

She loved it.

Zane was like a man possessed, driven to using what little time they had left together to bring her to the brink of pleasure and take her beyond. So far beyond that it was as if she had entered another dimension.

She thought he'd shown her everything there was to know about lovemaking.

She thought wrong.

There was so much more to learn, to experience. Zane made her body sing and her soul weep from the sheer pleasure of it. Like a guide who knew secret places unknown to the average man, Zane showed her about the parts of her body where ecstasy hovered, just waiting to explode.

Whitney gasped as Zane made love to her just by teasing the inside of her elbow, the back of her knee, the center of her instep with his mouth, with his tongue. She thought she would lose her mind if he continued. If he didn't take her there and then.

It was all, she discovered, the beginning overture before the symphony got under way. She'd been bent on arousing him, but in comparison to Zane, she was a hopeless amateur. An apprentice to a position that he had held for a long time.

It was as if his entire body had been fashioned with lovemaking in mind.

Zane used his lips, his teeth, his hands to bring her from climax to climax. He began cautiously, as if testing various theories he formulated in his mind. And proceeded with more and more fervor.

Each step took him closer to his goal. Each area he conquered paved the way to the next.

She was limp, her limbs liquid and useless, when she realized that he had replaced his hands with his lips. Her body jerked to attention. When his mouth claimed the essence at her very core, she thought she couldn't bear it anymore.

The sweet agony was overwhelming her even as ecstasy poured through her veins, waiting for one final release. And then it came.

"Stop," she whimpered. "I don't think I can take any more."

Zane raised his head to look at her, satisfaction glinting in his eyes. His own body was taut, waiting, hovering just on the brink. But he needed to do this, to get her to this place, to this edge where she now tottered.

She would remember. No matter what else would eventually crowd back into her head, he vowed to himself that Whitney would remember this. And in remembering, in the secret recesses of her heart, maybe she would not hate him quite so much.

"Sure you can."

"No, really, I don't know if I can take any more."

His heart swelled with love. "Okay, say uncle," he told her.

"Uncle," she exhaled.

He flicked his tongue and gloried in the shudder that went through her body. "Sorry, the password's just been changed."

"Uncle," she repeated. "Aunt, cousin, sister, mother, father—" Whitney surrendered. She was going to die here, on this floor, and she couldn't think of a better way to go. "Oh, the hell with it."

"Not hell. Heaven."

She was gasping for air as she felt his weight shift again.

When she opened her eyes a hundred years later, Zane was over her, as he braced himself on his hands, his arms on either side of her.

His breath teased her face. She could feel her body tingling. Waiting for him.

"Want me to stop?" he asked. As if he could.

Whitney didn't know where she found the strength, but she did. Maybe she'd been reinvigorated by his ardent lovemaking—she didn't know. All she knew was that she wanted to be one with him, to feel him inside her. To share the ultimate gift a man and woman could share.

"You do and I'll be forced to kill you." She said it so seriously that he almost laughed out loud.

"Can't have that." And then the next moment, he felt himself a prisoner again, completely captivated by the love he saw in her eyes. A love he had fooled her into thinking she felt.

A love he wanted to claim as his own.

She opened for him. Her breath stood still in her lungs as she held it, waiting. Very slowly, deliberately, he entered, his eyes holding hers.

"I love you," she whispered.

"I know." And that was his guilt, his burden. He'd made her love him when she wouldn't have, if she had known. "And I love you." He framed her face with his hands. "Remember that."

He said the oddest things at the oddest times, she thought. But she didn't have the energy to ask him why. She needed it for other things now.

Winding her arms around his neck, Whitney began to move with him. A second ago, she'd been too exhausted to even breathe on her own, but now she wanted to be with him on this final step of the journey, to use her body to bring him up and over just as he'd used his for her pleasure.

Hips locked, they moved in an escalating pace that swiftly catapulted them over the tip of the highest mountain. And then they were falling, embracing to protect each other from the impact. The ground far below was rushing up to meet them. It was lined with the soft leaves of spring, and when they finally fell, it cradled them with the warmth of a loving parent.

Zane remained over her a long time, aware that he

was probably crushing her. But he was unwilling to feel the slight breath of air along his chest that would signal the final separation of their bodies.

He didn't want to let her go. Not yet.

Not ever.

"Zane?"

The sound of his name rippled along his chest. His arm tightened around her in protest. But he knew he couldn't hold back the inevitable.

"Hmmm?"

She could have stayed like this until her golden anniversary. Maybe longer. "Do you think we could tell Quinton we died?"

He laughed. Shifting, he kissed the top of her head, then lay down on his back. He tucked her against him. "I don't think he'd believe us."

"We could try."

"Shh." He kissed her again, wishing there was some way he could prevent what was going to happen. "Just stay there a minute. I want to hold you a little longer."

They were lovely words, words to cherish. But they were motivated by something. Something she didn't want him facing alone.

Euphoria slipped away, edged aside by concern. She rose to look at him. His eyes wouldn't lie to her. "There is something wrong, isn't there?"

Zane stared at the ceiling. "No."

She didn't believe him. "There's something dangerous about working for Quinton, isn't there?" she pressed. Why wouldn't he trust her with the truth?

He couldn't just remain lying here, no matter how much the idea enticed him. That wasn't how things were done.

"Only if he feels his luck's been tampered with.

Speaking of which, we'd better get started.'' He sat up reluctantly. ''If we're not there, he's going to feel jinxed—and then he might cancel our deal.'' She nodded behind him. ''Want to take the bathroom first?''

Whitney rose. There *was* something he wasn't telling her. She had no doubts that he probably thought he was protecting her, but she didn't want to be protected. She wanted to be there to help him shoulder whatever was thrown his way.

It was just going to take a little time for her to get him to trust her. And undo whatever impression she had made on him before the accident.

''Sure.''

Not bothering to pick up any of her clothes, Whitney walked into the bathroom. Maybe she would think of a way to get Zane to open up to her while she was showering.

Chapter 13

Whitney sat in an armless, gold-and-green brocade chair that had been drawn away from the playing table and placed against the wall. It was an extra and so was she. Her adrenaline had been running high all evening. It warred with the need to remain as unobtrusive as possible. That was what she had promised when she had been ushered into the room.

She hadn't the knack that the waitress and the butlers had developed. They did their jobs and withdrew without making anyone consciously aware that they were even there. They were close to invisible in this room where only men and women with money were allowed.

Here there was no soft, piped-in music as there was in Quinton's suite of rooms. Music would only distract the players from their five-hundred-dollar-minimum-bet game. Even the air moved lazily through the room, in contrast to the energy she knew had to be pumping just below the surface within each player.

Her back was beginning to ache. The chair was not the most comfortable, designed to keep people at attention. She'd been sitting here for the past three hours, watching fortunes change hands in a blink of an eye. The drink that the waitress had brought her had long since become watered down, its ice cubes melting into the amber liquid, replacing the little she had sipped.

Tense, she wrapped her hands around the purse in her lap. She wished she'd brought the other one. It had beadwork she could have run her fingers along to distract herself. But Zane had asked her to bring this one, saying it complemented her ruby red dress. She wouldn't have thought he cared that much for fashion, but she supposed that he wanted everything to be perfect this last night with Quinton.

At least she hoped it was the last night. With any luck, after tomorrow, she would never have to see Richard Quinton again, barring perhaps a dinner party. She could not force herself to relax in his company. Beneath the charm and the good looks there was ice, sheer ice. She didn't trust a man with no heart.

Whitney shifted in her chair, crossing her legs, careful not to make any noise. Sally had not come tonight. Whitney wasn't sure if she was glad. It would have been nice to have someone to share this ordeal with.

But then, Sally wasn't exactly a soul mate.

Maybe it was better this way, Whitney mused. Conversation, if not expressly forbidden, was frowned on.

How much longer were they going to play? She doubted that Zane would even notice if she slipped out. As long as she did it quietly. But Quinton would notice. He'd been very specific about her remaining, as well as where. He wanted her to sit to his left. So that was where the chair had been placed.

She looked around the room with its golden leaf chandelier and heavily paneled walls. It had an Oriental flavor, from the wall coverings to the table to the rug. It was all so tasteful and all so cold. It felt like a tomb. An opulent tomb.

A modern-day equivalent, Whitney thought, of what the Egyptian pharaohs had requested for their final resting place.

The thought played over again in her head. Where had that come from? Whitney's heart beat a little faster. Maybe it *was* coming back to her. Maybe her memory was returning in increments, the small, insignificant pieces of information first. She knew that she didn't quite feel like an empty slate anymore. There was writing on the slate now.

But the only words about Zane were what had been inscribed in the past four days.

She looked at him. She wanted more. Much more. Though the past few days had been nothing short of fantastic, Whitney wanted her life back, her memory back. She wanted to remember meeting this man who was now sitting opposite Quinton, coolly holding cards in his hand. She wanted to remember the thrill of his first embrace, his first kiss.

Whitney smiled to herself, replaying the afternoon in her mind. She supposed, in a way, she already had that. Because of the amnesia, when he'd kissed her, it *had* been the first time. When her memory returned, she'd have each memory twice.

But what if it didn't return? What if she never remembered?

Would that be so bad? She knew she had a wonderful man in her life and apparently an exciting, unorthodox life-style. She glanced about. How many other women had managed to walk through these doors?

Beyond them, just a few yards away, were the penny-ante rollers. The tourists out for fun and the diehards who scraped together a meager stake and came to make their fortunes at the gaming tables. All of them would have blanched had they witnessed a single bet placed in this quiet room.

She'd blanched herself when Quinton had insisted that Zane play with them. The other men at the table had silently nodded their assent and Zane had appeared willing enough to join in. Only she had been uneasy.

During their stay—the part she could remember, she amended—she hadn't seen Zane place a single bet, pull a solitary lever or watch the tiny white ball jump over the grooves as the wheel turned with anything riding on it. Apart from watching Quinton play, he didn't appear to even be mildly interested in gambling. Was he a gambler, after all?

What else of consequence didn't she know about him?

Whitney moved to the edge of her chair as another round of bets began. The stakes for this game were already incredibly high. During the course of the evening Zane had appeared to hold his own. Was he good at poker or just lucky? Could they afford to lose the money if he wasn't?

When they had begun, Quinton had offered to stake him, but Zane had refused. Whether it was because he thought Quinton actually expected him to carry his own weight, or because he really did have money to burn, Whitney didn't know.

She didn't want to guess.

The headache that had sent her from Quinton's suite

this morning returned, wrapping steely fingers around the crown of her head.

Whitney tried to concentrate on Zane and not the pain. Edginess dampened her hands. She wished they had allowed her to stand behind Zane, but the players had all been in agreement with Quinton and relegated her to the sidelines, like the chair or an empty glass.

Even Zane had said she'd be a distraction. Quinton had said nothing about her presence bringing him luck this time, but he had appeared displeased when, between hands, she had suggested leaving for a while.

"You will remain, Mrs. Russell. And cheer us on." It was a blatant order. She had felt herself bristling, but in the end, for Zane's sake, she had acquiesced.

She hoped it wouldn't be much longer.

The room had been intended for private games of baccarat, the game of choice for most of the world's high rollers. But Quinton preferred the earthier feel of poker. So that was the game they were playing tonight. The table, with its inscribed patterns, had been covered, the design cleverly concealed with a specially created attachment the casino had made to please Quinton. The table cover seemed a small enough investment if it meant keeping Quinton happy. It was nothing in comparison to the price tag on the room itself, but even that had been inconsequential to the owners in the larger scheme of things. Over the life of the game, the saying in Las Vegas went, the house won.

The house was winning pretty consistently tonight, she noticed, much to Quinton's displeasure.

There was tension in the quiet room. She could see it, smelled it. It oozed from the players' very bodies, though they hardly moved, hardly gave any indication that this was more than a friendly game.

Friendly games were not devoid of conversation. Friendly games didn't have enough money in any single pot to supply food to a South American village for an entire year.

Her stomach began to turn, not from the tension, but from the waste.

There were eight men at the table, counting Zane and Quinton. Luck had initially kissed Quinton's cheek, but then capriciously gone on to flirt with two of the other men before returning to Quinton's side.

The return had been temporary. The Western-attired sheikh was showing a particular flare for the game. He'd won the last two pots. With a five-thousand-dollar minimum to get in and bets at five hundred or more, each had totaled over a hundred thousand. The chips were gathering around the sheikh in multicolored towers.

Unlike the dealer for the house, the sheikh was not winning graciously. As each hand brought him victory, he laughed, rubbing his hands together. The ruby on his left hand was the size of a walnut. It caught the light from the chandelier and blazed like fire captured in a setting.

The sheikh's small eyes glittered as he smiled broadly, stacking his latest win around him. He took particular pleasure in mocking Quinton.

"Ah, perhaps you should try your hand at something else? The one-armed bandits in the lobby might be kinder to you." Another, deep-throated laugh accompanied the suggestion.

There was no other sound within the room. The three butlers standing at the walls, trained to be guards as well as servants, had all but faded into the decor until needed. Their expressions remained completely impassive, as if they were not allowed to hear what was being said. Only their eyes indicated that they were alert.

Whitney held her breath as she watched Quinton's expression darken at the disparaging comment. She could almost hear the sizzle of the fuse as it was being lit.

Quinton glared at the sheikh. A little of his polish slipped. "Why should I settle for a one-armed bandit when I can play with one who has two?"

The rage in the small dark eyes was immediate. Whitney could have imagined the sheikh threatening Quinton for the audacity of his words.

The sheikh's temper was barely controlled as he demanded, "Are you challenging me, Mr. Quinton?"

Quinton's mirthless smile returned. He'd accomplished what he wanted—to get under the other man's skin. It was little enough to ask in exchange for the sum he had lost.

"Just making an observation."

Afraid of an escalating confrontation, one of the butlers left his post and came forward. He placed his gloved hand on Quinton's shoulder. The next moment, a look of horror crossed his lined face. Whitney guessed that in the intensity of the moment, the man had forgotten his place.

Her sympathies were instantly aroused. Whitney exchanged looks with Zane. Almost imperceptibly, he moved his head from side to side. He didn't want her saying anything.

Quinton jerked his shoulder away, even though the butler had immediately removed his hand. His face twisted until his expression bordered on malevolent.

"Get me your manager."

"Right away, sir."

The game was suspended as the pale butler withdrew, backing out of the room as if he were taking leave of royalty.

For all his airs, Quinton was slime. Very polished, educated slime. Zane glanced toward Whitney, his eyes slipping to the purse on her lap. He would have preferred if she wasn't almost a room length away.

No one spoke a word in the few minutes that they waited for the casino manager's appearance. The agitation on Quinton's face was plain. The others at the table seemed either amused by the incident or sympathetic toward him. To a man, they all had their own superstitions and taboos to deal with. Luck was a capricious enough commodity without having obstacles placed in its path.

The reason for the butler's approach in the first place was forgotten. The sheikh had melded into the background of observers, waiting for the drama to play itself out.

The manager, Harry Goodman, appeared quickly. He was never far from the room when a private game was in progress. Keeping things running smoothly was what he was paid to do. That and entice the high rollers to either return to Zanadu, or forsake their previous hotel affiliations whenever they were in town.

From Goodman's sickly pallor, Whitney judged that the man did his job around the clock and it was taking its toll.

Entering, he went straight to Quinton. Goodman's manner toward him was politely authoritative yet subservient at the same time. Zane watched and marveled, wondering if there was a school somewhere that taught how to project that manner. And how to walk upright while seeming to bow.

Goodman, a thin, bald man in his early forties, inclined his head. There was the proper degree of respect in his voice as he asked Quinton, "Is there a problem, sir?"

"Yes, there's a problem." Quinton didn't even bother looking at the butler, who stood several steps to the rear of Goodman. "He touched me. I specifically said no one was to touch me during a game."

Disgusted, Quinton abruptly rose from the table. The chips closest to the edge tottered, then spilled down, a shower of blues and golds spreading along the richly carpeted floor. He glared accusingly at Goodman. His losses during the course of the evening had placed him more than a million dollars in debt, a great portion of that to the house.

Losing always enraged him. "My luck's ruined for the evening. The game is over."

Goodman knew better than to argue with him. A man's luck was precious, and if he felt it had turned sour, then there would be no coaxing him back to a table until such time as he felt it had changed.

Perspiration appeared on the manager's brow. Whitney began to feel sorry for him. And to really loathe Quinton. But at least the torture of watching Zane play was over.

Zane rose. He had lost more than he had won, but the overall impact had not been too great. It helped not to be playing with his own money. Quietly, he came up to join Quinton. The man hardly appeared to notice. His attention was focused on Goodman and the butler.

The manager looked around the table to see if any of the other players could be subtly coaxed into remaining. But the atmosphere in the room had altered, and all thought it was best to call it a night. They could return tomorrow, when luck had had sufficient time to reaffirm its loyalties.

There was bad karma in the room now. Gamblers knew better than to come up against bad karma. No one was the winner then.

"Very well, sir." The manager signaled for the other butlers to begin clearing the room. To him remained the task of having Quinton make good on his marker. His experience with the man had taught him that if Quinton didn't settle up within twenty-four hours, collection might take anywhere from six months to a year, if at all.

If he'd had hair, it would have long since turned gray.

His job, at the moment, was to make himself available to Quinton for as long as the man needed. Quinton had lost a considerable sum. Provided that he made good the debt, Zanadu would eagerly await his return. All that meant smoothing over any hard feelings.

He hurried out of the room in Quinton's wake, subtly elbowing Zane out of the way. The latter, he knew, was only in the entourage of a high roller, not one himself. Goodman had been around the breed long enough to know the difference.

"I'm very sorry, sir. It should not have happened. I assure you that the man will be severely reprimanded for his thoughtlessness."

Quinton stopped in the lobby, turning on his heel. The look on his face was so dark that Whitney found herself pitying Sally tonight.

"I want him fired," Quinton retorted. "He ruined my luck and my evening and I want him fired. Do I make myself clear?" Though they were of approximately equal height, Quinton gave the appearance of being taller than Goodman. And far more lethal. "Not transferred, not talked to, not docked. Fired. Tonight."

"Sir, please—"

Quinton was unmovable. Not even the fear he saw in the other's eyes diverted him. His losses had been too great and too irritating.

"Tonight," he growled.

Defeated, Goodman surrendered. "It'll be taken care of."

Incensed at the injustice and appalled that a silly superstition could cost a man his job, Whitney opened her mouth to intervene. She had no idea what she was going to say, only that she wanted to let Quinton know how small a man she thought he was.

She felt Zane's fingers press warningly on her arm, aborting her words before they had a chance to form.

Whitney blew out a breath, annoyed that Zane didn't rise to the occasion and that he didn't want her to, either. She hadn't thought of him as a moral coward. But then, Whitney reminded herself, she really didn't know him, did she?

Quinton waved the manager away. Goodman withdrew, clearly grateful to be out of the line of fire.

It was redirected at Zane. Whitney could almost feel Quinton reloading. "So, where were you?"

Zane did his best under fire. "Right across from you, Mr. Quinton."

Quinton didn't know if Russell had guts or just mush for brains. "You two were supposed to be my good-luck charms. Maybe you're getting a little tarnished."

Did that mean that they were free of this ridiculous obligation? Whitney certainly hoped so. "You can't really think that we brought you luck, or that that man touching you jinxed it." To her it was all a ploy on Quinton's part, an excuse, a way to blame others for what went wrong.

She didn't realize what she was up against. "Whit," Zane warned.

"I have more money than the entire population of Rhode Island. That gives me the right to think any damn thing I please." Taking a breath, Quinton appeared to temporarily check his anger. Frowning, he looked out at the casino floor, not seeing any of the crowd that was milling around. "When a man's luck changes, he's got to change some other things to make it come back." Quinton turned to look at them pointedly.

It sounded like a convoluted philosophy, but Zane knew that Quinton believed it. He was beginning to get that itchy sensation at the back of his neck again.

"Such as?" Zane asked guardedly.

Quinton's eyes turned steely. They were eyes that could appreciate the beauty of a fine, rare painting or a sunset. They were also eyes that could watch a man twist and squirm, pleading for his life. Eyes that could watch a man die.

"Our deal," he replied coolly.

Zane braced himself. "You want to terminate it?" He was going to have to do some fancy talking to change Quinton's mind. It couldn't just all go up in smoke now. Not after all they'd been through.

"On the contrary, I want to escalate it." Quinton's eyes shifted so that they were exclusively on Whitney. "Tonight."

She didn't understand. What was going on? How could the deal go through tonight? Weren't they talking about developing Quinton's property, building tracts of homes on it? How could any of that be settled tonight?

Zane's mind began to race. He had to get in contact with Sheridan. "I don't have the money here."

His smile was cold. "We've already established that. But it is somewhere else, right?"

Though he was looking at Quinton, Zane was not oblivious to the fact that the man's two bodyguards were moving closer. "Yes."

"Where you can get your hands on it." It wasn't a question. It was a command.

Zane felt his throat growing dry. This was going sour. He had to get Whitney somewhere safe. "Yes."

The smile on Quinton's face turned ugly. "Then I suggest you get your hands on it."

He wasn't ready for it to be tonight. Everything was set for tomorrow at noon. Somehow, he was going to have to bluff his way out of it. Zane reached for Whitney's hand.

"All right, I'll just—"

Quinton's hand was faster. He caught Whitney's wrist, pulling it out of Zane's grasp.

"Get your hands on it for me," Quinton concluded. "And I'll just hang on to the little lady for safekeeping, if you don't mind." He spared Whitney a smile that cut right to the bone. "Just until you and Taylor return with the money." The man who answered to the name Taylor took a step forward, waiting.

Quinton's suave smile returned as he curled his fingers around Whitney's hand. "It's not that I don't trust you, Russell, but a man in my position has to take certain precautions, you understand. After all, luck still might be running against me."

Whitney tried to pull her arm away and couldn't. Quinton's grip was too tight. She wasn't frightened. It hadn't occurred to her yet to be afraid. She was confused. And concerned about what Zane had gotten himself into.

There was guilt in Zane's eyes when she looked at him. Her heart sank. "Zane, what is he talking about?"

Confident that things were going his way, Quinton could afford to become charitable again.

"Luck, my dear. That whimsical thing that can make a beggar a king or a king a beggar. I don't like being a beggar." He motioned Taylor forward. "Take him where he has to go and don't let him out of your sight. I want you both back here within an hour." The tone remained light, the message no less deadly. "One hour, that's all you have, Russell. After that—"

Quinton didn't have to complete his sentence. The gleam in his eyes said it all.

Zane's mind, always so orderly, threatened to desert him. All he could think of was that he had placed Whitney's life in jeopardy. Exactly what he had been trying *not* to do by keeping her in the dark.

"How do I know I won't just be handing you the money?" Zane demanded. "How do I know I'll be getting something in return?"

So he did have a backbone, after all. Quinton's laugh dismissed the question. "And here I thought we were developing such a friendship. You have my word, Russell." He stroked Whitney's arm. "And I have all the cards, as it should be."

Quinton looked at his watch. "Now I suggest you get going. Time is ticking away."

What was the hurry? What difference could a few minutes possibly make to Quinton one way or the other? Zane knew the answer even before he formed the question. It was because Quinton enjoyed making people dance to his tune.

"What if I can't get to the money and return within the hour?" Zane challenged.

Whitney had never seen a colder smile. Finally wakened, fear began to crawl up her spine.

"I wouldn't ask such questions, Russell," he warned, "unless you have a stomach for the answers. When I feel unlucky, I become very nasty. It would be a shame to expose your wife to such nastiness, but then, it's out of my hands."

It was all Zane could do to keep from wrapping his hands around Quinton's throat. But venting his rage wouldn't settle anything. And it wouldn't help Whitney.

Whitney couldn't stand being in the dark any longer. "Zane, what is going on?"

Zane tried to keep his concern from registering on his face. "It'll be all right, Whitney." *I swear it'll be all right.* He took a chance and tried to reason with Quinton. "Look, she doesn't know anything. Let me take her with me. You can still send your man with us to get the money."

"What money?" Whitney cried. Her question was all but drowned out by the collective din around them. "I thought he was paying you."

Quinton laughed. "I guess she really doesn't know anything. Commendable, Russell. But she still remains with me." His hand tightened around Whitney's arm. "Think of her as an insurance policy. If everything is as it should be, there's no reason for you to be concerned. If not..." His voice drifted away and he shrugged carelessly. "Well, that'll be on your head. Now, I would advise you to hurry. Traffic might be difficult this time of the evening." He raised a hand, signaling for his other bodyguard. "Reese, have the hotel bring the limousine around."

His attention returned to Taylor. "And for heaven's sake, if Russell winds up taking you to another hotel, don't have Zanadu's chauffeur whining about it.'' He could have been a simple businessman, complaining about shabby tactics as he looked at Whitney. ''They get so possessive just because they swallow a fifty-thousand-dollar tab. If you so much as look at another hotel, they think you're taking your gambling there. It's worse than having a jealous lover.''

How had Zane gotten mixed up with someone like Quinton? The man was vermin. ''How difficult for you,'' she felt compelled to say.

He laughed at the obvious loathing in Whitney's eyes. He liked a woman of spirit. He'd sensed it about her almost from the first. Quinton could feel his appetite getting whetted.

Taylor began ushering Zane away. ''Whitney,'' Zane called to her, ''it's going to be okay.''

But how could it? she thought. How could it when she didn't know what ''it'' was? After four days, she was back to square one, completely confused about her life and the man who was in it.

Numb, she didn't remember walking to Quinton's suite. She'd placed one foot in front of the other and somehow arrived there.

With a deceptively gentle hand around her shoulders, Quinton guided her into the living room. The butler closed the door behind them. The remaining bodyguard took his position before it.

Whitney looked around. There was no one else in the room. ''Where's Sally?''

''She's been dispatched home early. There were a few things I wanted her to take care of for me.'' He could read her mind. It empowered him. ''You needn't be afraid of me. Unless your husband doesn't return.''

A reserve of courage fortified her. "He'll be back, and I'm not afraid."

"Brave words. We'll see." Quinton gestured toward the bar. "Can I interest you in a little champagne? Or are you still drinking mineral water?" He chuckled. "Oh, my, I seem to recall that we've had this conversation before."

He was laughing at her. She didn't care. All she cared about was Zane. "I think I'll have a Scotch and soda."

The request for the bracing alcohol came from deep within, from a region Whitney hadn't been able to unlock from the outside. She needed something to steady her nerves.

Quinton laughed, pleased with the choice. "You surprise me, my dear. I would have thought a light wine would have suited you better."

Her first impression had been right. Beneath the impeccably tailored clothing and smooth manner, Quinton was a pig. A pig with a well-oiled veneer.

She raised her head defiantly. "You don't know anything about me."

"On the contrary, my dear, I know all I need to know." Raising a glass, he toasted her.

The irony of it was, she thought, he probably knew more about her than she did.

Chapter 14

Whitney sat on the sofa, poised like an arrow ready to be released from a bow. She struggled to make sense out of what was happening.

The facts refused to arrange themselves in any semblance of order.

Racked with tension, she was pressing her wrists against the purse in her lap so hard that it was digging into her thighs. She ignored it, ignored everything but the icy feeling running along her spine.

Her hands were wrapped tightly around the chunky Scotch glass. *Please, there has to be good explanation for this. There has to be.*

Her throat felt dry, parched. It wasn't anything the drink could remedy. Whitney forced the words out. "You don't really have a piece of land you want developed, do you?"

This had to be how a deity felt, Quinton thought. Trifling with people, moving them around like so many chess pieces on a board, for amusement. He was enjoying himself again.

"On the contrary, I hold the deeds to a great deal of property, Mrs. Russell. Both developed and undeveloped." He rose and poured himself a drink. "As well as controlling interest in a great many businesses on both sides of the ocean."

Quinton's voice was coming from behind her. She resisted the temptation to turn around and look at him. That was what he wanted, to be center stage. It was a small thing, but she refused to indulge him.

After a beat, she asked, "Which ocean?"

He took his whisky straight up. Swallowing, he let the alcohol course through his veins, invigorating him. "Pick one. I'm almost respectable, you know. Which allows me to do what I want, when I want."

He was smug. She had a feeling that as long as he felt he was in control, he could be lulled into being too self-confident, a little lax perhaps. It might make the difference between being able to get away and not.

Quinton felt he was in control? her mind mocked. Quinton *was* in control. Complete control. It was hard not to let that unnerve her.

What was he doing back there?

Tension was making her back and shoulders ache. Whitney stared straight ahead at the water as it cascaded down the fountain. "What is this all about?"

His laughter mocked her question. "You really don't know, do you?"

She felt like a fool. A hopelessly blind fool. How could Zane have put her into such a position? But he had and she was going to have to work with that.

Whitney drew her anger around herself like a mantle. "Would I be lowering myself to ask if I did?"

"Lowering yourself? Is that what you consider it?" Quinton turned the phrase around, examining the sentiment behind it. "No, I don't suppose you would 'lower' yourself, as you put it, if you did know." Just the slightest hint of grudging admiration entered his voice. "Russell's better at keeping secrets than I gave him credit for. Another man, in the throes of ecstasy, might have told you everything."

Standing directly behind her, Quinton bent over and whispered into her ear, "Did you take him there, into the throes of ecstasy? I'll bet you did."

He saw the tension dancing along every fiber of her body and it pleased him. Nursing his drink now, Quinton moved around the sofa until he was in her line of vision again. There was loathing in her eyes. He respected hatred. Took it as a compliment and an affirmation. People hated what they feared.

His eyes were darkened with lust. "With that fine, upstanding attitude, and that tight little compact body, I'll bet you're a very passionate woman once the door is closed." His eyes shifted to the door behind her, as if he didn't already know that it was closed and the room secured. "My door is closed." He caught his tongue between his teeth as he regarded her. "Why don't you give me a preview? I might even find it in my heart to tell you a few secrets myself."

She held herself rigid, afraid that if she didn't, she would shiver. Whitney didn't want him to know just how urgently fear was beginning to lick at her.

Disgust filled her eyes. "I don't want to know that much."

He laughed, amused rather than affronted. Knowing he could dispose of her like a used tissue at any time he chose added to his enjoyment. He continued toying with her.

"Liar. You're consumed with curiosity." His glass nearly empty, he sat down beside her. One arm was carelessly thrown over the back of the sofa, hemming her in. "Despite my losses, I'm feeling rather generous tonight. Perhaps it's the company."

Setting his glass down on the corner of the beveled-glass table, Quinton placed one manicured hand over hers in an intimate move that made her skin crawl.

His eyes slid over her. Whitney could almost feel them peeling her dress off.

With a jerk, she pulled her hand away. Something dangerous flashed through his eyes, then left. The realization struck her that here was a man who could kill instantly, without compunction or remorse. She had to be crazy to challenge him.

"What would you say if I told you that you're married to a drug dealer?"

The question hit her with the force of a physical blow. She felt as if she'd just stepped on a land mine. "I'd say I didn't believe you."

He shrugged and turned his attention to his glass. The two fingers' worth disappeared easily. "Whether you believe it or not, it's true."

Quinton was just saying this to upset and confuse her. Why, she had no idea. Maybe he enjoyed torturing people. "Zane is a land developer," she insisted.

The man had done a good job of covering his tracks, Quinton thought. He could use a man like that. Maybe he'd change his plans for Russell, after all. But that remained to be seen.

Right now, he diverted himself with bursting the bubble around this woman.

"He's a lie developer. His kind will lie, cheat, steal. Sell out their own families for next to nothing." Quinton contemplated his surroundings. Surroundings he had earned, in his own fashion. "I should know, my dear. Those are my roots."

He gestured around the room with his glass. There was unmitigated pride in his voice.

"Not bad for a drug dealer from Liverpool, is it?"

She had to keep him talking, to distract him until Zane returned. Zane would make some kind of sense out of this for her.

"You're British?" Then the slight trace of an accent she'd detected hadn't been an act. It was real.

The corners of Quinton's mouth curved slightly, giving him almost a Satanic appearance.

"I prefer to think of myself as a citizen of the world." It was a fact that he was welcomed anywhere. As well as feared. Nothing gave him greater satisfaction. "The world is a great arena to deal in, provided you have something they want." And Quinton had always made certain that he had that in his possession.

Such as now.

Shifting, he ran his fingers along her bare arm, then laughed as she stiffened. She'd come around, he thought. Everyone always did. And if she didn't, it made no difference. He'd take her, anyway. He fancied a blonde tonight.

"As I said, I'm considered respectable now." There was contempt for the word in his voice, as well as for the people who kowtowed to him. "But the lure, oh, the lure of danger keeps bringing me back to renew my spirit."

He was crazy, she thought. Absolutely crazy. She began to seriously fear for her own safety, and for Zane's. "You disgust me."

Quinton snorted. "Fortunately, I don't care." Quinton glanced at his watch. "Your husband has a little less than twenty minutes left." He wanted to watch her squirm, to sweat out the minutes. To know that he could do anything he wanted with her. "You don't think perhaps he's had second thoughts, do you? Given my man the slip and cut his losses?" She was resisting the idea, but he could see a kernel of it had found fertile ground. "That would mean that I retain custody."

Her head jerked up. Zane had to come back for her, he had to. He wouldn't just leave her with Quinton like this.

How much did she really know about him? a small voice inside her whispered. Not much. Maybe nothing, but she knew this. Zane would be back for her.

"Custody of what?" she demanded.

Guts, she had guts. She was foolhardy, but she had guts. And she'd fight him off like a wildcat. He was going to enjoy her.

"You."

She could feel chains snapping around her wrists. This was no time to fall apart. She had to think, to resist. "I don't know about the rest of the world, but slavery's been outlawed for more than a hundred and thirty years here."

Her scent had been tantalizing him for the better part of the past hour. Mixed with fear, it was almost overpoweringly irresistible. He could feel himself growing more aroused by the moment. There was nothing like closing in on a prey.

Quinton moved closer to her on the sofa. "There are many forms of slavery, my dear. Slavery to a substance." He toyed with the ends of her hair. "To a woman."

Whitney rose to get away from him. "To superstitions."

Rather than become enraged or embarrassed, he laughed at her obvious ploy. His observance of his superstitions were what had brought him to this point in time. To where all the cards were his to play.

"Touché. We'll see in twenty minutes whether or not you've managed to enslave your husband or not. Oops," he mocked as he glanced at his watch. "My mistake. Make that seventeen minutes now. They're just slipping away, aren't they? Well, you know how time flies, Mrs. Russell, when you're having fun." Reaching, Quinton tangled his fingers with the hem of her dress. "Would you like to have fun?"

Whitney yanked the fabric from his grasp. She felt caged, helpless, and it galled her until she could hardly breathe. Mechanically, she slipped her purse's thin gold chain on her shoulder. It swung against her side as she moved.

"What do you know about him? Zane. What do you know about him?"

He enjoyed breaking down whatever lies Russell had fed to his wife. Quinton pretended to think before answering.

"All I need to know. That he's done well for himself rather quickly. He has a reputation of selling only the highest-quality cocaine. Which is why his path has brought him to me."

Still holding her drink, she looked at the vase on display just a few feet away. "Is that supposed to impress me?"

"Yes." Quinton followed her line of vision and knew

just what she was contemplating. "I wouldn't try to throw that if I were you. My reflexes are undoubtedly a great deal faster than yours, and it would be a terrible waste of good art."

Whitney thought she was going to be ill.

She didn't want to believe Quinton. It could still all be nothing more than lies. It had to be. Even though what he told her made the pieces fit together better. The deceptions she'd caught Zane in. The evasions every time she asked Zane a direct question. That was the behavior of someone with something to hide.

Whitney pressed her lips together. She stared at the rings on her left hand. The diamonds blurred in the haze of tears she fought to keep back. Her eyes burned. She'd fallen in love and married a man who was the lowest life form on the earth.

No! Her mind screamed. It had to be a mistake. Quinton had to be lying. There had to be another explanation for this.

Didn't there?

She was beginning to believe it, Quinton thought. He could read it in her eyes. When he rose, crossing to her, she didn't move.

"It's all beginning to make sense now, isn't it?" Quinton's voice was almost kind. "You know I'm telling you the truth." He urged the drink she was holding up to her lips. "You're not the first woman to find out that her husband's lied to her. And I can show you a perfect way to get revenge."

Something snapped to life within her. This was what he was trying to do, this was why he was lying. To turn her against Zane. And get her to go to bed with him.

His hand was over hers as he coaxed her to drink.

Whitney twisted the glass and flung its contents into his face.

Like an explosion, rage instantly transformed his features. Whitney saw the fury in his eyes at the same moment that she felt the sting of his hand across her face. Stumbling backwards from the force of the blow, she tasted a trickle of blood seeping into her mouth. He'd cut her with his ring.

And he was coming after her. "You miserable, stupid wretch!"

The door opened just then. His hand raised to strike her again, Quinton turned. "Knock!" he roared at the intruders.

Taken by surprise, Taylor looked from his boss to the woman. "I brought him back."

The rage she'd seen on Quinton's face was nothing compared with what she saw on Zane's as he hurried to her side.

"What the hell are you doing to her?" Zane demanded. He was going to kill the bastard with his bare hands, to hell with the consequences.

Quinton composed himself. Women weren't worth getting angry about. "Repaying her for my impromptu shower." He took out his handkerchief and wiped his face.

Holding her chin in his hand, Zane examined the cut on Whitney's cheek. There were no words to describe the guilt he felt.

"Are you all right?"

She didn't know whether to melt into Zane's arms or to run from both of them. Whitney knew what she wanted to do, but that was just her heart talking, not her head. Maybe if she'd been thinking instead of feeling, she wouldn't be here like this.

"I don't know." She looked at Zane, silently pleading for him to tell her that everything Quinton had said was a lie. "Am I?"

She knew, Zane realized. Or thought she did. He should have told her what was going on. But it was too late now.

"This is all very touching," Quinton commented, "but boring." He was beginning to lose his patience. He stared at the small, black valise Zane was holding. His question was addressed to his bodyguard. "Does he have it?"

The barrel-chested man came forward and nodded. Russell hadn't let him see the contents of the case, but why else would a man keep a valise in a hotel safe unless there was something worth stealing in it?

"Yeah," Taylor answered.

"Good." Quinton turned his attention to Zane. No, he wasn't going to groom him, after all, he decided. To have a successor meant that there was always someone waiting for you to die or abdicate. He intended to do neither for a long time.

"Then I'll take it." Eyes fixed expectantly on the valise, Quinton put out his hand.

Zane didn't relinquish the case to him. Instead, he slipped his arm tightly around Whitney. They were only ten feet away from the front door, but that meant going through Quinton and two bodyguards. The den, with its bay window, was twice as far away. Right now, it represented their only chance.

"Where's the cocaine?" Zane heard Whitney's sharp intake of breath, felt her disappointment as she stiffened beside him. It went through him like a sword thrust to the hilt.

Quinton's patience was at its breaking point. He smiled, but his expression was malevolent.

"Oh, I'm sorry. Didn't I tell you? There's been a slight change of plans. Due to my losses at the table tonight, I've decided to keep it all. My drugs and your money. You've let me down and displeased me." He spread his hands wide. "Fortunes of war, I'm afraid. If you don't give me any trouble, I might consider letting you both go."

Zane knew they had only a few minutes to live. Taylor was already reaching for the weapon beneath his jacket. He only hoped Whitney was up to this.

"All right," he agreed. "No trouble. It's not worth it." Stepping forward, he began to give Quinton the valise, then suddenly rammed it against the man's midsection.

Caught off guard, Quinton fell backward against Taylor. The latter's half-drawn weapon discharged against his own chest. With a gasp of sheer terror and surprise, Taylor fell to his knees. Dead. A red splotch on his jacket was growing wider even as he fell.

Zane never looked back. Grabbing Whitney's hand, he yanked her toward the den.

"Move! Move! Move!" Like the burst of a discharging automatic weapon, he shouted the command at her.

Running on disembodied legs, Whitney found herself being propelled into another room. The den, from the looks of it. Zane slammed the door shut and flipped the lock.

That wasn't going to hold, he thought.

Trembling with the realization that everything she'd put together over the past few days was falling apart, Whitney could only stare at Zane. "He wasn't lying. You are dealing in drugs."

This was no time for true confessions. "We'll talk about this later, okay?" Grabbing a chair, Zane threw it against the window, shattering it. "C'mon, we have to get out of here."

Not waiting for her to comply, he pushed her through the broken window just as the sound of gunfire erupted behind him. The next moment, the door was flying open. Zane ducked as he dove out behind Whitney.

A bullet whizzed by his head, narrowly missing him. He hit the ground running and grabbed for her purse, yanking it away from her.

Whitney spun around in time to see Zane pulling a small revolver out of the purse he had insisted she take with her.

She hadn't opened her purse the entire evening. During all that time, the gun had been just sitting there and she didn't know.

But Zane had known.

He'd known this was going to happen and he hadn't told her. A man didn't put a woman he loved in jeopardy. Whitney felt as if her very heart was being ripped out.

She looked as if she was in a trance. "Run, damn it," Zane ordered, turning to fire at Reese, Quinton's bodyguard. "He's going to kill us."

The explosion echoed around her. The next moment, she saw Zane drop to the ground, clutching his arm. There was blood everywhere. Zane's blood. Whitney thought she cried his name, but she wasn't sure. She wasn't sure of anything. It was as if she'd been dropped headfirst into a chute, a time tunnel where everything went whizzing by her.

Images formed and reformed in her mind. Her lungs

felt as if they were bursting, as if she'd run a great distance.

But rather than run, she snatched the revolver from Zane's hand. Holding her breath, she fired, point-blank, at the man charging at her. The man who had shot Zane.

A look of pure amazement creased his wide face as Reese looked down at the hole that had formed in the center of his chest. He was still staring it as he crumpled to the ground.

Before. She'd done this before. Held a gun aimed at a man. And fired.

She bit back a cry of anguish as everything turned dark. Whitney fought hard against letting it overwhelm her and swallow her up.

When her vision cleared, Quinton was standing in front of her, his gun aimed at her head.

He had just moments before others would come, crawling around the scene. Just moments to reap satisfaction. He meant to have it. And then he would buy his way out, with money and blackmail, as he had done on several other occasions in the past. He wasn't worried, only angry.

"You surprise me, Mrs. Russell. You have more courage than I thought. And more brains." His eyes shifted to take in the gun in her hand. "I should have thought to have your purse searched."

Taylor had searched Russell before the game as a precaution. But it hadn't occurred to him that the woman might pose a problem.

Quinton shrugged. "My error. Now I'll take that, please." One hand out to her, he smiled confidently. He saw how her hand was shaking.

Physically ill, Whitney thought she was going to dissolve right where she stood. Her hand was shaking not from fear but from sheer anger. And her head ached so that it was almost blinding her. Beside her, Zane lay on the ground. And one man was dead.

Her stomach knotted as she raised her hand and wrapped it around the other. The small barrel still wavered.

"No," she whispered hoarsely.

"Oh, the hell with it."

She saw it in his eyes a split second before it happened. Saw what he meant to do. Firing straight at Quinton, Whitney fell to the ground, her body partially covering Zane's. The impact made her drop the gun. It went sliding along the concrete, out of reach.

Quinton's bullet went sailing over her head, hitting the air where she had stood only a moment ago. Missing its target.

Her bullet didn't.

She heard the sirens in the background as she raised her head to look at Quinton. He was struggling to get up, blood pouring through his fingers from his shoulder where her bullet had struck. Whitney immediately scrambled to her feet, but there wasn't anything she could do. The gun was out of reach.

Quinton raised his gun. "I should have killed you immediately instead of waiting."

The weapon was aimed at her at point-blank range. She was going to die.

Whitney closed her eyes to shut the sight out. The click of the hammer screamed in her head, melding into the sound of the gun being discharged.

She didn't feel anything.

The sound of a body hitting the concrete had her eyes flying open. As if in slow motion, she saw Quinton crumpling at her feet.

"I guess this is a day for surprises." They were his last words.

Stunned, Whitney looked around. Zane was on his knees behind her. Reese's gun was in his hand.

She ran to him. There was so much blood everywhere. How much of it was his? Using her shoulder as support, she helped Zane to his feet.

"Are you all right?" she asked.

He wanted to pull her into his arms. To assure himself that she was safe, after all. That he had managed to save her.

"I've been better." It was an effort to talk. "You?"

Whitney could only nod numbly. "I'm okay." And then she raised her eyes to his. "Zane, I remember. Everything."

Chapter 15

Within moments, they were surrounded by noise and people. Whitney started, braced, then relaxed when she saw that it wasn't Quinton's people but her own arriving on the scene.

A dark-haired man she recognized as the waiter who had told Zane that he had a telephone call at poolside was the first to appear.

Adams, she thought his name was. He was a rookie at the Justice Department. She had five years on him. No, five and a half.

Behind Adams arrived others. Within minutes, the area was filled with squad cars and an ambulance. In the background, she thought she saw the hotel manager being held back by a policeman. He didn't look very happy.

Small wonder, Whitney thought. Goodman had just irrevocably lost one of his high rollers. That left him with almost a million-dollar debt that would remain unpaid, and a suite of rooms he would have to redecorate before anyone would want to stay in them.

She made out other faces in the crowd.

The policemen on the scene were unknown to her, but the men in suits weren't. They were all part of the same operation. Her operation. Hers and Zane's. An operation that had been two years in the planning and six months being set up. It was a sting intended to bring down one of the most devious suppliers of drugs on the West Coast. A man whose position in society and influential friends, coupled with an effective method of covering his trail, had aided him in eluding detection. Up until two years ago.

But his luck had finally run out. Done in by his good-luck charms. It seemed poetic somehow, she thought.

Everything was coming into focus again. So quickly that her head was beginning to ache.

Bill Sheridan, the man she and Zane worked for, bent over Quinton. He laid two fingers against the man's neck and grimly shook his head. He would rather it had gone down a different way, but there was an up side to Quinton's meeting his demise like this.

"Well, you two just saved the taxpayers some money. He's not going to be standing trial." Rising and carefully wiping his fingers to remove the taint of touching Quinton, he focused on the pair. Zane was still leaning against Whitney.

Sheridan signaled for a paramedic. "Over here!" He had to shout to be heard above the din. "Lucky for you Adams saw you being hustled from the hotel by Quinton's bodyguard. He followed you in his car and called me. I radioed for backup."

Zane nodded, only partially hearing the information.

Sheridan turned around, impatient. "I said, over here. I've got a man down."

"Not down," Zane corrected, trying to smile. "Just a little bent."

His shoulder felt as if it were on fire and it hurt like hell, but there was something more urgent on his mind than his arm. Whitney's memory had returned. It seemed as if everything about this whole operation had been just beyond his control once it got rolling. He hadn't wanted her to find out on her own that he had purposely kept her in the dark, not without warning. Above all, he didn't want her to think he had manipulated her.

He looked at her. She was pale. "You remember everything?" he asked, hoping against hope that somehow the situation wasn't as black as he knew in his heart it was.

She could feel the wounds opening within her. Big, gaping wounds. And they all had Zane's mark on them. She'd trusted him more than she had ever trusted anyone. How could he have betrayed her like that?

How could he have allowed her to make love to him under false pretenses, when she didn't know what she was doing? When she wasn't even in her right mind?

She raised her chin. "Everything."

Relief washed over Sheridan's patrician face. "Does this mean your memory's back? I don't mind telling that you really had me worried."

It was obvious that Sheridan, at least, was delighted. That made one of them, Zane thought, mentally kicking himself for waiting too long. She was going to hate him for this now, he thought. He'd never seen such hurt in her eyes.

"Yes, it's back." Whitney changed the subject. She didn't want to talk about her amnesia. Or the stupid things she'd done while walking around in a daze. They'd haunt her enough as it was. She nodded toward Quinton. "We didn't get the cocaine." Her voice was matter-of-fact, terse. "We never had the opportunity to make the exchange. Quinton got greedy after his loss at the tables and wanted it all." She frowned, remembering the look in the man's eyes. That, too, was going to haunt her for a long, long time. "And me."

Sheridan nodded, listening. "Can't say as I'd blame him for that," he interjected.

Bantering came easily to her. It was one of the things that had made her so acceptable to the rest of the group, a group that was composed predominantly of men. But this time, Whitney ignored her superior's comment. The less she thought about this venture, the better. She couldn't wait to start putting the whole episode behind her.

She went on talking as if Sheridan hadn't said anything. "So I guess all we managed to do was cut off one head on the monster, but not its heart." They'd hoped for names in exchange for leniency. Names and locations. Now all that was lost.

Sometimes it felt as if all they were doing was running frantically in an ever-turning wheel, just trying to keep their balance. She watched as two paramedics zipped the body bag closed and strapped Quinton onto a gurney. This part, at least, was over.

She raised her eyes to Sheridan. "Another head will pop up to take its place by the time we all get back to L.A."

Cutting off the various heads, as she put it, was the name of the game. For the time being, it was the only way they could keep from being completely overrun. But

Sheridan did have a piece of good news to give her that might help ease things.

"Maybe not that quick." She looked at him quizzically. "We've got more than you think."

The hotel had remained under constant surveillance, thanks to the bugs Zane and Whitney had managed to plant, and it had paid off.

"We have Quinton's mistress. Picked her up just as she was getting ready to board the plane for New York." Sheridan was very pleased with himself. "Seems after we had a nice, long chat, she was very eager to talk in exchange for immunity." He laughed, rubbing his hands together. "She's also a hell of a lot smarter than Quinton obviously ever gave her credit for. I don't think he would have kept her around if he'd known just how sharp she was and how much she really knew about his covert operation."

"No," Zane agreed. "He liked them dumb and willing." He glanced at Whitney. "Present company excepted, of course."

Zane had made love to her, taken advantage of her. The thought was still twisting like a knife driven straight into her gut. "Oh, I don't know, present company can be pretty dumb at times."

She wasn't just poking fun at herself. There was something in her tone, a distance that had never been there before. The old Whitney wasn't back, after all, Zane realized. She'd sent a completely different emissary in her place.

He wanted to talk to her, to straighten things out. To pick up the threads of what they'd had before the fabric was completely unraveled because of his mistake. "Whitney—"

Finally free, one of the paramedics came over to Zane.

Whitney stepped out of the way as the man moved between them. She didn't want to hear anything that Zane had to say. There wasn't anything he *could* say.

"Get yourself taken care of. You're bleeding all over the place. You know how hard it is to get blood out of silk?" Whitney turned toward Sheridan. "Want a full report tonight?"

He shook his head. She looked beat. Judging by what had gone down, it must have been a hell of a night for her. "It can wait until morning. Why don't you get yourself cleaned up?"

Whitney mechanically dragged a hand through her hair. "Yes, maybe I should." At least she could take a shower. The rest of it, well, it was going to take more than water to clean that up.

Bone weary, she turned away and began walking to the hotel without a backward glance.

The paramedic was still busy working on his shoulder, impeding him. Zane moved his arm away. "Give me a minute," Zane insisted when the paramedic protested.

"But your shoulder—"

Zane ignored him. The bandages could wait. Whitney couldn't.

"Whitney," he called as he hurried after her.

She wanted to keep walking, walking until she disappeared. But she didn't want a scene, not in front of everyone, so she stopped. Shoulders stiff like a Marine in formation, she stared straight ahead of her.

"What?"

She wasn't turning around. But she wasn't running away, either. Maybe that was a good sign. Zane hurried over to her, holding on to his arm. It hurt with every jarring step he took. Other things hurt more.

When he reached her, she finally looked at him. The

look was cold, removed. As if she could just barely tolerate the sight of him. The trouble was, he couldn't blame her. Zane's mouth felt dry. Where the hell did he begin?

With the truth, he suddenly realized. If he had any chance at all, he had to lead with the truth. Even if he started with something small.

He searched her eyes, looking for an opening. There was none. "Whit, I don't know what to say."

Her expression completely shut him out. "Obviously. You've already proven that. Look, unless you want to have a commendation posthumously awarded, I'd get myself back to that paramedic, if I were you."

He wasn't about to die, at least not from the flesh wound Quinton had given him. "Whit—"

She didn't want to hear it. Didn't want to hear the sound of his voice anymore. She'd behaved like a fool and he'd been privy to that. All she wanted to do was crawl into a hole and die.

"I'll see you later, Russell." With that, she walked quickly away, the sound of her heels against the concrete echoing into the night.

Zane could feel each step as if it had been taken right across his heart.

Sheridan came up behind him. "She doesn't look like a woman who just narrowly escaped with her life and wrapped up an important case in the process," he commented thoughtfully.

Zane didn't feel like getting into it. "There are extenuating circumstances."

Sheridan raised a brow. "Problem?"

Zane stood watching, even though she had disappeared. "You might say that."

Sheridan didn't believe in interfering in his people's

personal problems. And he didn't believe in those same problems interfering with work. "I also might say fix it. And I will. Fix it. By morning if you can." It was a direct order. "And get that thing bandaged. I can't afford to lose any men. The department spent too damn much money training you."

"Yes, sir," Zane murmured, still looking after Whitney. What the hell was he going to do now?

Zane remained standing outside the hotel door a good fifteen minutes after he'd gotten off the elevator. All fifteen minutes were spent trying to get his courage up. He'd rather have faced another bullet than the hurt look in Whitney's eyes, knowing he was responsible for putting it there.

He thought of knocking, but that would give her an opportunity to tell him not to come in. He used his key instead.

Whitney jumped when she heard the door opening. Some federal agent she was, she upbraided herself, picking up the pair of shorts she'd dropped. As skittish as a wet-behind-the-ears rookie. More.

She had one of her suitcases open on the bed and was packing. There was a pile of clothing on the bed. The closet stood open and empty, except for the wedding dress. It was conspicuously hanging there, like the one child not picked for a baseball game when sides were being divided up.

He tried his best to sound nonchalant. "What are you doing?"

She barely glanced in his direction. It took effort just to look cool.

"Not very observant for a federal agent, are you?" she commented. She tucked in a pair of shoes beneath a dress in the case. "I'm packing so I can get that out of the way. I'm leaving first thing in the morning, after I make my report. What I can remember. Of course," Whitney continued, refusing to look at him, "there're still some gaps, like how I really got amnesia."

"I was supposed to place a bug in Quinton's suite. You insisted on coming with me. We were almost done when we heard someone entering the suite. We were on the second floor. The safest way out was the balcony. When we shimmied down the side to the ground, you fell the last six feet and hit your head. You told me you were all right, but I made you go to the emergency room, anyway. The doctor there thought you were all right, too. He was wrong." Zane blew out a breath. "It was my fault. I shouldn't have let you come with me."

It was coming back to her fuzzily, but she could remember. "Last time I looked, you didn't have any authority over me. As I recall, I'm the one with seniority."

He held up two fingers. "Two weeks." That hardly qualified her to pull rank. He watched her place the suitcase beside the bed. It was now or never, before he lost his nerve. "Whitney, we have to talk."

She spared him a glance, but even that was too much. It hurt to look at him. To see the face of the man she had finally allowed herself to love, only to wake up and discover that it had all been a sham. And, most likely, a joke.

"Yes, we do," she agreed tersely. "When we get back, I'm putting in for another partner."

Her decision stunned him. They'd been partners ever since he'd arrived at the department. They'd shared each other's life, been each other's backup. She was his best friend and he hers. How could she decide to just arbitrarily throw all that away without even talking to him about it?

"What?" he demanded.

She wasn't going to cry. Splitting up was for the best. If anything like the word *best* could be applied to the situation.

"Well, in light of what's happened, we can't go on working together. Okay?"

She was cutting him off at the knees and sending him on his way. Well, if that was what she wanted, he wasn't going to oppose her.

Zane nodded. "Okay. Okay," he repeated quietly as he crossed to the door. He needed a drink. A tall one. Maybe several.

His hand on the doorknob, Zane suddenly swung around. This was all wrong. He wasn't going to get pushed out. Not anymore. "Damn it, it's not okay."

She raised her head and looked in his direction. "What did you say?"

Zane strode back across the room. The volume of his voice increased as he came closer. "I said it's not okay. We're not going to back away from this like we did before."

Stunned, she stared at him. "What are you talking about? What 'before?' There was no 'before.'"

If they were close, it was as friends, not as lovers on the brink of something serious. No matter what she might have felt in those secret moments when she lay alone in bed at night. She was too well-trained to have allowed anything to happen between them, to give in to her own feelings and suffer consequences. She was happy just being his friend.

And now, they weren't even friends.

It was time for truth on both their parts. "Wasn't

there?'' he demanded, his eyes pinning her down. ''When we first met? Wasn't there something?''

She tossed her head, looking away. ''I don't know what you're talking about.''

Zane circled so that she was forced to look straight at him. ''Then maybe your memory hasn't returned completely.''

Whitney gritted her teeth. Why was he badgering her like this? What did he hope to gain? She pulled out the second suitcase and threw it on the bed. ''Or maybe yours is a little off.''

He wasn't wrong about this. ''I don't think so. There was an attraction between us. At least there was on my part.''

''Yeah, right.'' Much as she had wanted it once, she would be a fool to believe him.

''There was.''

His voice was so low that she stopped packing and turned around to look at him. She wanted to believe him, but she knew better. ''Then why didn't you ever say anything about it?''

The answer was simple. He'd felt her out and she had deliberately not seemed interested. ''I was afraid of getting laughed at.''

People knew better than to laugh at Zane. ''By who?'' she scoffed. ''The guys?''

''You.'' He knew he had her there. ''You were one of the guys. You worked so hard at blending in, at being 'one of the guys' that I thought—well, I thought you weren't interested.'' She'd made it clear just where the lines were drawn between them and what side he was to remain on. He'd settled for her friendship and the fact that he could always rely on her.

She didn't believe it, not for one minute. She couldn't

let herself. That would make her twice the fool. "And you quickly drowned your sorrows in another woman." Whitney paused, as if thinking. The figure was on the tip of her fingers at all times. Because it hurt. "By my count, you've had eight in the past six years."

And none of them had meant anything for even five minutes. He'd assumed that no woman ever would. "Doesn't that tell you anything?"

She went back to packing. She couldn't look at him anymore. "Yes, that you're fickle."

He grabbed her by the arm and forced her to look at him again. "That I haven't found the right one. And the reason for that was because none of them were you."

For a second, just a second, she had trouble catching her breath. If she were to believe that…

But no, she knew why he was saying that. "If you're trying to justify what happened here—"

She couldn't be that dense, he thought. She had to be doing this on purpose. "I'm not trying to justify it. I'm trying to make you understand why it happened."

He wasn't going to talk his way out of this. The least he could do was not spin any stories and admit like a man what he'd done. Like the man she'd once believed was her friend.

"I know damn well why it happened!" she shouted. "It happened because you were leading with your shorts again and you saw the perfect opportunity to take advantage of me." She pressed her lips together, refusing to cry. "And I didn't make it very hard for you."

It was the first truthful thing she'd said so far. "As I recall, you were throwing yourself at me."

She shrugged. "Yeah, well—"

With his finger beneath her chin, he lifted her head. He saw the tears shimmering in her eyes. It would have hurt less if she'd hit him with a two-by-four. "And I wasn't taking advantage."

She swallowed the tears that were coating her throat. "Then what would you call it?"

"Being lucky."

She jerked away. She might have known. With shaky fingers, she picked up a nightgown. It was a scrap of blue gauze, meant only to be seen as a prop if Quinton had his men search their room. But she had worn it to seduce Zane. Her cheeks flamed with embarrassment.

"Getting lucky. Same thing."

"No, it's not." He pulled the nightgown out of her hands and threw it aside. "Damn it, stop packing and listen to me."

She picked up the nightgown and refolded it, then tucked it into the suitcase. "I can do two things at once."

"Well, I can't." Uttering a ripe curse, he used his good hand to jerk her around until he had her attention. When he looked into her eyes, his anger melted. "I have cared about you, Whitney, for a very long time."

His voice was tender. How long did he expect her to keep her heart hardened? "I know, we're friends."

She was the most infuriating woman he'd ever met. And the most desirable. For both their sakes, he struggled to keep his temper.

"Yeah, we are. And as your friend, I want to tell you that your partner's in love with you."

Her mouth dropped open. "What?"

He repeated it slowly, letting each word sink in. "I am in love with you."

"I don't believe you."

He'd expected this. "That's always been your problem, running. And you're running again."

Whitney drew her brows together. What was he talking about? "Again?"

Zane nodded. "Just like you did in the beginning." He could see the riot of words forming in her mind. He wasn't about to allow her to let them loose. "When you lost your memory, you were different. Still you, but different. I don't know how to describe it—it was like—"

"I had no scruples?" she supplied. He'd made her feel wanton, reckless. And she'd loved it. But it had all been a terrible mistake.

"No," he continued patiently, though the denial was firm, "it was like you had this light that seemed to go off within you."

He wasn't going to talk his way out of this with pretty words. Having partnered with him for six years, she knew just how glib his tongue could be. "So now I glowed in the dark?"

"You're doing it again, making jokes, putting up defenses again just like you did before." He finally saw through her. Through the tough veneer, down to the woman who existed beneath. The woman he'd made love with. "What are you afraid of, Whitney?"

She sighed, dropping the last article of clothing into the suitcase. "You want to know what I'm afraid of? All right, I'll tell you. Getting my teeth kicked in. That's what I'm afraid of. That's what love does—kicks your teeth in and then walks away." She dusted her hands off and then snapped the locks into place.

This was something she'd never shared with him. While he had told her about the women in his life, she'd never mentioned men, except for a vague reference to someone important once being in her life. "Boy, you must have had one hell of an experience."

"Maybe."

It had been, and it had branded her for life. So much so that when she'd first met Zane, she'd purposely fought the attraction she'd felt. If it blew up in her face, working together would become hell. She liked him, respected him and didn't want to risk losing him because an affair between them hadn't worked out. She had banked down anything she'd felt and he'd remained in her life. If that was difficult at times, well, it was still worth the trade.

Or so she told herself.

"If I did have an experience," she hedged, "it taught me not to put myself on the line."

If she thought that, she was wrong. "You did it every day," Zane pointed out. "With me."

There was a difference. "I was protecting your life, like you were protecting mine. The heart had nothing to do with it."

He didn't believe her. "The heart," he insisted, "had everything to do with it. Those four days, when you didn't have all this baggage around to weigh you down, you were different, freer. You acted as if you loved me." And he had believed her. Because his act had been the real thing.

She tried to dismiss it. "I thought I was your wife."

He wasn't buying it. "No excuse. Lots of wives don't automatically love their husbands and you had nothing to fall back on, no memories. I even tried to talk you out of it when you thought we should be making love," he reminded her.

Whitney looked away. "More reason than ever to get another partner."

"Why?" he demanded angrily. "Explain this to me— I'm a little slow."

She blew out a breath. He was making this hell for

her. Why couldn't he just accept the break and let it go? "Because we can't go back."

She was afraid, he realized. Really afraid. That was why she'd gotten so angry, because he'd made her feel things, and now she was afraid of that. His anger disappeared, replaced by tenderness.

"Why should we?" He brushed his hand along her cheek and watched her eyes widen. "Why don't we just go forward?"

Just what was there to go forward to? "And what, be lovers?" she asked hoarsely.

For the first time since he'd entered the room, Zane grinned. "Sounds good to me."

Under ordinary circumstances, his smile would have curled into her being. She shut it out. "Well, not to me. What do we do once it's over?"

"You're terminating something before it's even had time to root. This isn't like you," he insisted. She was usually the optimist, the one who saw a rainbow behind every storm. Why was it so difficult for her to see the rainbow here? "And who says it has to be over?"

Just what was his point? "You're saying you want to be my lover forever? You, Mr. Flavor of the Month?"

He shook his head. "No, I don't want to be your lover forever."

There, he'd admitted it. "Then why are we even having this discussion?" Exasperated, she yanked the suitcase off the bed.

"Because I want to be your husband forever."

Stunned, Whitney dropped the suitcase. "What did you say?"

With his toe, he moved the suitcase away, giving him clear access to her. He slipped his one good hand around her waist.

Zane shook his head. "Twenty-nine years old and your hearing is going already. I hope you come with a warranty."

She doubled her fists and pounded him on the chest. He knew she was only kidding. Had she wanted to, she could have really hurt him. Having accidentally gotten in the way of it once, he knew firsthand that she had one hell of a punch.

"Can the funny stuff, Russell. What are you saying to me?"

She felt good like this. Against him. As if she belonged. "I'm saying that I don't want another partner. Ever. I'm saying that the room is paid up until the end of the week, so we might as well make use of it. I'm saying you've got a gorgeous wedding dress in the closet that's a shame to waste. I'm saying—"

"Will you marry me?" She didn't know if she was feeding him the line, or asking for herself.

His eyes crinkled in a smile. "Yeah, that too."

He wanted to marry her. He *really* wanted to marry her. And she wasn't hallucinating or struggling with another bout of amnesia. "Then say it."

Taking her hand in his, he looked into her eyes and asked seriously, "Will you marry me?"

Whitney raised her chin, an aloof expression on her face. "Well, I don't know—"

He laughed, encircling her waist and pulling her to him. He hardly noticed the ache in his shoulder. "Shut up and kiss me."

"Is it always going to be like this—you issuing orders?"

He thought about it. "No, sometimes you get to say shut up and kiss me."

Her eyes were shining with tears again, but they were

good tears, happy tears. He considered himself a modern man. He knew the difference.

"Why don't you?" she urged.

He wanted to be completely sure. With Whitney, at times, it was hard to tell what she actually meant. "Is that a yes?"

She took his face in her hands, her heart swelling. He did love her. It was going to be all right, just as he'd promised her it would be.

"If you don't know by now, partner, then I guess there're still a few things about me you're going to have to learn."

He grinned. "I'm looking forward to it."

The lessons began immediately.

Epilogue

She would have let him out of it. Whitney was so drunk on happiness and love that she would have let Zane out of his proposal for a while if he'd wanted it. She would have been perfectly content to savor the thought of actually becoming his wife. There was no real rush to make the marriage a reality.

But Zane didn't want out. He wanted in. And he wanted it all immediately. He wanted Whitney and all the trimmings that went with a formal wedding: the flowers, the music, the church, even the rice.

"They don't throw rice at weddings anymore," Whitney had pointed out during the long, elaborate negotiations they had conducted beneath the hotel's silk sheets as the euphoria of lovemaking held them, exhausted but contented, in its grip. "They throw confetti."

"As long as it's nothing lethal, I can live with it," Zane had concluded just before he found himself reaching for her again.

So it was settled.

Two days later, because Sheridan had connections that reached far and wide, Zane and Whitney found themselves exchanging vows before an elfin priest complete with an Irish brogue. The man couldn't have fitted in better with the scene than if he'd been sent over from central casting. He was almost *too perfect.*

As Zane caught Whitney's hand and she ran beside him out of the church, she made a mental note to have the priest's credentials verified. Just in case.

Outside the picturesque hundred-year-old church, an army of their friends and associates joined together for a single purpose. To pelt the newlyweds with tiny, multi-colored squares. The color began raining on them as soon as Whitney and Zane emerged from the building. It followed them on their run down the steps, to the curb.

But at the white limousine that was scheduled to take them to the reception hall, Zane held up his hand. After another thirty seconds, the hail of color subsided.

"I want to kiss my wife," he announced. "And I want to do it without risking getting a mouthful of confetti."

The announcement was met with cheers, hoots and a variety of noises that defied description or categorizing.

"How did Sheridan manage all this?" Whitney whispered to Zane. She was still stunned at the speed with which it had all been arranged. There was no three-day waiting period, no blood tests, nothing. Every obstacle had been circumvented.

Zane looked over her head toward Sheridan. "The man goes to great lengths to keep his people happy and working smoothly." He winked at her. "I think maybe he expects our firstborn in return."

Whitney laughed, throwing her arms around Zane's

neck. She didn't think it was possible to be this happy. "It *is* legal, isn't it?"

He grinned, pulling her to him. "Just try to get out of it and you'll see exactly how legal and binding it is."

"Maybe I will," she countered. "In about a hundred years."

"Sounds fair enough to me."

"Shut up and kiss her already!" Sheridan shouted at them. "You can talk later."

"I think our benefactor just made a request." Zane nodded toward Sheridan.

Whitney didn't even bother turning to look. She was too busy looking at Zane and feeling her heart swell. This time, there were no doubts, no worries, as there had been before. This time, it felt real. The love, the happiness, all real. "Always keep them happy—that's my motto."

"I try," Zane whispered against her lips just before he kissed her. "I surely do try."

"After all this, you'd better do more than try," she warned, a smile playing on her lips.

And he did.

* * * * *

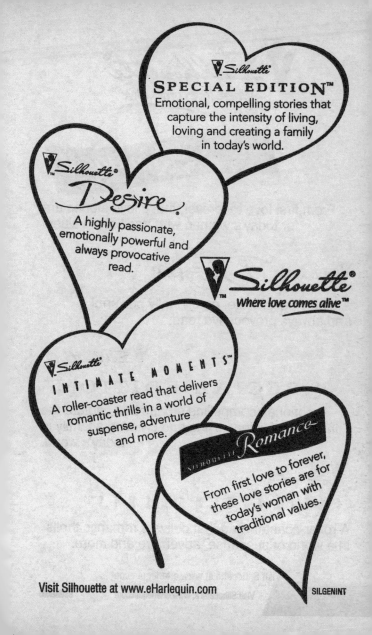

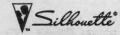